The Kingdom of Strange

Marshall Cavendish Corporation
99 White Plains Road
Tarrytown, NY 10591
www.marshallcavendish.us/kids

This book is a work of fiction. Names, characters, places, and incidents are products of the author's imagination and are used fictitiously. Any resemblance to actual events or locales or persons, living or dead, is entirely coincidental.

Library of Congress Cataloging-in-Publication Data
Klinger, Shula.
The Kingdom of Strange / by Shula Klinger. — 1st ed.
p. cm.
Summary: An English class project to find one's audience as a writer by posting original works on a blog leads fourteen-year-old Thisbe on a journey of self-discovery and new friendship.
ISBN 978-0-7614-5395-6
[1. Authorship—Fiction. 2. Blogs—Fiction. 3. Interpersonal relations—Fiction. 4. Self-perception—Fiction. 5. High schools—Fiction. 6. Schools—Fiction.] I. Title.
PZ7.K681Kin 2008
[Fic]—dc22
2007015853

The following quotes which appear in this book are in the public domain:
p. 42 from "Ozymandias" by Percy Bysshe Shelley
p. 87 from *Macbeth* by William Shakespeare
p. 212 from *Romeo and Juliet* by William Shakespeare
p. 231 from "The Eve of St. Agnes" by John Keats

Interior artwork by Shula Klinger
Book design by Vera Soki
Editor: Robin Benjamin

Printed in China
First edition
10 9 8 7 6 5 4 3 2 1
ᴍᴄ Marshall Cavendish

For G.P.H.

The Kingdom of Strange

a novel by
SHULA KLINGER

Marshall Cavendish

SUNDAY

Time to open a new file. Control-S. Done.

Mom and Dad have gone. Today ushers in the reign of Granny Ed and the Evil-Smelling Pooch.

I'm speechless.

Ok, not for long. Am extremely grouchy and even a good rant won't help. I'd talk to Fishbone, but in spite of his tremendous goodwill, he is still "only" a cat and therefore unable to contribute much in the way of verbal advice. He's also busy right now, contemplating the borders between the recently established Cat Zone and Dog Zone. The borders were Gran's idea. A way to keep the beasts separate until some kind of peace agreement has been reached.

Thisbe, STOP! Write something with a point to it.

Since this is a new file, I should introduce myself. I am an imaginative sort of person, I guess. You wouldn't call me "flamboyant," but I definitely think of myself as "creative." Genetically I am a combination of the fleece-and-corduroy combo (on my dad's side) and the Lycra People (on my mom's side). I don't like Lycra because it's sexy. I like it because it stretches and doesn't fight back when you put it on. I am a bit lazy about my appearance, but I prefer to think of myself as "relaxed."

I do fine in school. I don't stand out but I don't let myself fail, either. With two parents who've been in school forever, I would never live it down. My hair's a disaster and I have mostly given up on it. Unlike my clothes, my hair's been putting up a good fight for years. It actually won years ago, but my friends (or the people who I thought were my friends) never told me. I do not dye my hair blond or iron it flat every morning, like they do.

I love pizza. I don't buy slices; I eat the whole thing. I worship at the temple of carbohydrates and celebrate the tao of toast (or is that "taost"?). I hate meat.

I keep to myself at school, but my mind is a buzz and jumble of hundreds upon hundreds of stories. Teeming, breeding stories that chatter to me and to one another, rearranging their characters and climates and geographies . . . their societies and centuries and cosmologies . . . at the same time. I am an honest person and would never tell a lie, but my brain is Story Central, churning and bubbling in a big saucepan. One day I'll serve up such a steaming, hot bowl of wickedly nutritious Story Soup that I'll be famous. Just wait.

One of my favorite places to make up stories—or watch them happen, since that's how it feels—is on the bus. I'll sit on the swaying, rattling bus, watching a woman with a sheltie puppy on her lap. The woman spends the whole journey trying to stop the dog from chewing on the large leather buttons on her jacket. I make a mental note of the woman's expression. She's not aggravated but she's firm. The right adjective can be found later.

That's when I start to wonder. I take the adjective-less expression and turn it over in my mind, wondering about the old coat with the big brown buttons. It's vintage, surely? Maybe it belonged to her mother? Maybe this woman—let's call her Elizabeth—lost her mother many years ago and describes her, even now, as a mystery: a woman whose cautious spirit never quite inhabited her body. She never really knew her mother, did she? Wait! Maybe she only wears clothes that once belonged to her mother. Perhaps I might marry Elizabeth to Thaddeus, a man whose personality could be compared to "a dangerous undertow."

And then I will get distracted because there is a girl about three or four years old kneeling on a seat on the other side of the bus. The girl spends the journey trying to work out how the panels of the bus fit together, tracing every screw and joint with her finger.

These elements—these people, dogs, and buttons—drift through my journal every day, as stories without endings. In my own mind, I call them "bustories," but I've never mentioned this to anyone else. I write in my journal constantly. "Religiously," my dad says. I hate that. I tell him it's not worship; it's a visit.

So, Elizabeth and Thaddeus: Welcome to my journal! How do you like it in here? You are just one tiny sliver of the story pies that fill my day. Now that I've started writing the slices down, I really want to share them.

Somebody might like what I write. But who can I show my writing to? I want someone else to read my words. But not these ones! I live in mortal fear of someone else reading my journal.

Dear Reader (unless you are me, but slightly older):
STOP READING AND CLOSE THIS FILE!

Now to my purpose:

AUDITION LIST
Role: My Reader
<u>Melinda</u>: No!

<u>Kel</u>: No no no no noooooooo

<u>Mom/dad</u> (for they are as one flesh): Definitely not

<u>Mr. Oliver</u>: 10 out of 10 as an English teacher. Zero otherwise (and especially in the clothing department)

<u>Granny Ed</u>: Dad's mom, recently arrived from Seattle with stinky pooch in tow: EEK! No way

I must be a good writer. So many "inventive and surprising" ways to convey a simple no. That's what last year's English teacher put on my report card: "Inventive and surprising." What did she mean? That I surprised her by writing in a language I'd invented? She must have got a little giddy with the thesaurus.

Since I've already introduced myself, I guess I should say something about my girls. Melinda and Kel. They have been my friends for years, but lately things have been weird. We used to be like three superheroes, or prima ballerinas, or an all-girl band, or little detectives solving terrible mysteries together. We slept over at Kel's and toasted marshmallows in her fireplace when it rained on Halloween. Melinda loved to eat. It was first on her list of "10 Things I Love." We all made those lists. For Melinda, "eating" came way above "ponies," "butterfly barrettes," "new ballet shoes," and "anything yellow." We hung out in her kitchen and made cookies. Or we made the dough and ate the whole bowl of it raw. Felt sick for days. Melinda and I went to ballet lessons together. That's where we met Kel. I always thought it would be more fun to stamp my feet instead of pointing my toes, but I went along with it I got into tap dance later.

We were an excellent team. Melinda with her long blond hair and delicate, dramatic limbs. She looks like a pale, icy pixie with a pointed chin and quick movements. Then there's Kel with her dark hair in a bob. Her whole head of chestnut hair swung together like glossy fabric when she twirled in dance class. She's shorter than Melinda and her face is rounder. She doesn't say much. She's like Melinda's shadow, in all senses. And then there's me. The third amiga with the big head of crazy hair, brown eyes, and short limbs that I can fold up really, really small when I'm watching people and I don't want them to notice. Which is quite a lot of the time.

But let's be clear about this new Era of Weird. It didn't begin with one of those fights you see in the hallway at school. Nobody yelled. Nobody pulled anybody's hair. Nobody slammed a locker door and accused anybody of kissing her boyfriend, or spreading rumors, or "looking at her funny." Nobody threatened to kick anybody's *ss, and nobody had to go and get a teacher. In other words, there have been no cosmic explosions. Our friendship just seems to be drifting and dribbling away into a distant black hole in the strange solar system that is high school and the after-school universe of endless reality TV shows.

Oh no. I hear Granny Ed and the Evil-Smelling Dog. Better sign off and patrol the borders of Cat Zone.

Week One, April 2

MONDAY

Monday morning again, and it's another English class for the ninth graders. The teacher, Mr. Oliver, notices that Thisbe is trying to pay attention, but she looks preoccupied. Maybe something happened before class? He hopes it wasn't serious. She is a good student, and he doesn't want to see her wander.

Today the class is starting a new assignment. The theme is "Audience." They're going to look at stories from the reader's point of view. The students will work in pairs or groups on the same story. They'll read the story or watch a movie adaptation of it, and then explore their reactions to it as its audience. Mr. Oliver says the students should take some risks, be creative, and write their responses in whatever form they want. The finished project is due on the last day of class.

There's also an online option, if they wish, with the students at another school. Ms. Patinsky teaches ninth grade at Westerley High. If they want to collaborate with her students, they should refer to Option b in the handout they're about to get. He points to a Web address on the whiteboard.

Mr. Oliver expands on his subject: Who is the audience of a story? Does the author always know? Can you tell from the way a story is written? Who do you think J. D. Salinger had in mind when he wrote <u>The Catcher in the Rye</u>? *Are you the reader he imagined? Why or why not?*

Thisbe looks up when her teacher mentions J. D. Salinger. She catches his eye only for a second. She's a wonderful writer, and he wants to keep an eye on her. He wants to keep an eye on David, too. David looks a little distant today, wearing headphones around his neck and one of his vintage gas-pump attendant shirts. Having a bad day? Everyone else just looks blank, even the ones taking notes. One kid in the back is spinning his pencil as he lies almost horizontal in his chair, with one leg flung out into the aisle.

There's the bell. Time to wrap up.

Audience Assignment
Mr. Oliver, English 9
Johnson High School

Introduction:
In this team project, you will have a chance to consider a novel or short story (or movie adaptation) from your own point of view. I'd like you to start with these questions:
• Which novel or short story have you chosen and why? Tell me about the main characters and their situation/conflict. What is interesting about them?
• Where and when is the story set? Whose point of view do we see? (e.g., Is there a narrator?)
• Who is the intended audience of this piece? How does the author's view of his/her audience determine the language, setting, characters, etc. of the story?

What to do next:
Option (a):
• Please read/view your story and write in your project journal, either during or shortly afterward. Talk to friends and family about your reactions to this work. How did it make you feel? Why did you care about the characters? I want you to think about yourself as a member of the author's audience. Why might this book have been written for you?
• Explore the idea of Audience however you like. How does the audience bring meaning to a story? How is the audience different for a novel, a movie, or a play? Can the audience determine whether or not the story is a success? How?

Option (b) Online:
• The same guidelines apply, but your team members would be posting comments to a blog that I've created with a Westerley High English class.
• You may share your words and email addresses, but no photos of yourselves, no home address/telephone numbers, etc. Your messages will be plain text—but I am confident that you don't need all that fancy formatting to create magic with your words.☺
• To contribute to the site, please go to the address I gave you in class. Your first task is to post a message introducing yourself.

How you'll be marked:
• Title or question: 10%. Come up with a brief, focused question or title for your project. Extra points for wit and ingenuity, I promise.
• Project development: 20%. This mark is for all decisions, activities, and teamwork. This includes communication with me about challenges/issues and communication with your team members. If you need help at any time, please ask (instead of festering quietly in a corner . . .).
• Presentation: 20%. Please share your favorite moments from the story and why you have chosen them.
• Final report, including project journal: 50% (or stun me with your brilliance and we'll talk about bonus points). **You have 12 weeks to complete your mission. No late assignments, wimping out, or pathetic excuses, please.**

Mr. Oliver handed out a new project today. We are supposed to do this project in groups. We can also do it on his blog, but I don't think any of the other contestants were interested in door number two. There certainly won't be any surprises about the groups people choose. I already heard Melinda and Kel arranging their little twosome. I have decided to work online; I don't care if everyone else thinks it's geeky. This project is a good idea. It could be interesting to talk to students at another school. Otherwise you start thinking that this school is the whole world. That this is all there is and that these people are so important. Hmm. Maybe if you took all these smart, shiny people and put them in another school, they might not look so great. They might not be powerful. They might NOT be cool.

Today was particularly weird. Out of the blue, right after lunch, Melinda and Kel started calling me Frisbee. Literally at the same moment, as if they'd decided to do it together. They know I hate it. They know that kids in elementary school called me Frisbee to tease me. Right after that, I sat next to Melinda in Mr. Oliver's class while she was doing her smiling, fake I'm-so-interested-please-give-me-an-A thing. I couldn't help myself. I wanted to turn around and poke her with my pencil. HARD. I should have been able to think up something funny and cutting to say back to them, but I couldn't do it in class. That would be stupid. About as stupid as calling me Frisbee. Why do they think it's funny, anyway? All I could say was, "My name's from a BOOK, dummy!

You'd know that if you'd ever finished reading a book in your life!" and then I felt worse. Fighting with your friends is so pointless. I mean, you should fight with enemies, right? Which makes me wonder. What does that make Melinda and Kel?

I should focus now, and follow Mr. Oliver's instructions to post on his blog. I did my best to keep the assignment paper safe between two books, but it still got squashed. Looks as though the books were having a fight over who got to eat it first. So, I smooth it out with my hands and fold back the corner that was chewed off in the battle. Ok, here we are, at his address. Hmm. Nice template, Mr. Oliver. I wonder if you picked that green and orange border. Looks remarkably like the color scheme on one of your less well-chosen garments, if I may say so.

Time to be brave and introduce myself. Name? Thisbe. Comment? Here goes.

◇ ◇ ◇

At 4:30 PM on April 2, Thisbe said:
Hi everyone! My name is Thisbe and I'm at Johnson High School. I would like to use this site to share my writing with an Audience. I've never done that before. I'm looking for some honest (but gentle!) criticism to help me kick off my brilliant career as a novelist. ☺ Thanks for reading—see you online!
Thisbe

◇ ◇ ◇

<u>Later today:</u>
Where is everyone? When do I get my chance to be inventive and surprising? I'm stopping by every hour, but the only message there is mine. I have twelve weeks to finish this assignment, and if it goes on like this, there won't be much to say. I really hope someone else logs in.

I'm going to write in my journal and keep the discussion site open in the background. Oh, my journal. My habit, my passion, my obsession, my prized possession. I have written in a journal since I was nine years old. I have spent five years, or approximately 260 weeks, on this particular project so far (sure beats anything Mr. Oliver could give us in English!). It has traveled through many notebooks before it reached its current status, as a well-stocked folder on my hard drive. I spend hours writing in it, itemizing and recording observations about the world, the people I know, and their funny habits.

At this time, I'm mostly writing about myself. Long, rambling essays. I didn't use to—which is just as well—but I have been very preoccupied lately. And now, with my parents away, it makes a great escape from Granny Ed and her evening walks with Chutney. She's staying here for three whole months and I've been *dreading* it. I have never been alone with her for that long. That's another 77 dinners, 78 breakfasts, and 22 lunches with her until my parents get home. I think.

At 6:30 PM on April 2, Thisbe said:
Hello everyone! Thisbe here again. That's Thisbe as in THIZ-Bee. I would really like to share my writing with someone. I write poems and lots of stories, but I never finish them—and I NEVER share them. If I knew I had an audience for my writing, I might actually finish something! Could you be my audience? If you join me in this project, I promise to be unusually brave and listen to your comments on my work. We could write up my stories and your comments as our final project. What do you say?

Thisbe

TUESDAY

Fishbone is keeping me company. It's nice. He usually goes out at night, but with Mom and Dad away, I think he's freaked out. He sat by the front door when they came down with their bags on Sunday. Just looked at them with his big, desperate eyes, twitching the end of his fluffy tail. It was kind of pathetic until I noticed that he was sitting on the mat (the mat is No-Man's-Land, i.e., both Cat Zone and Dog Zone). Hey! The cat sat on the mat. I don't think he saw the humor. Fishbone is a superior feline, but even he doesn't make jokes. It is his only shortcoming.

Mom and Dad must have called about sixteen times before they got to the departure gate. You'd think I didn't even know where the fridge was. I'll be fine. Peanut butter is food. Frozen waffles are a meal. And with Granny Ed here, I won't have a minute to feel lonely. And then there's Chutney (Dog-Smell Central). It definitely won't be quiet. . . . I could actually do with some loneliness after two weeks of Dad being SO perky about his trip, trying to decide which of his ugly sweaters he should take with him (none of them, I suggested helpfully). And he kept making terrible jokes that attack so fast you can't hide when you see them coming. They just smush you in their stupidness. I'm annoyed just thinking about them. He laughs, wahahahahaha, all pleased with his joke, and my mom shakes her head. Why does she put up with it? I hope he gets whatever it is out of his system while he's away. Then he can come home from England all de-stupidified and be my normal, quiet dad again.

RANDOM THOUGHT: When do fathers stop dressing well? Were they fashionable once? When do they drop off the edge of the fashion radar?

While my folks are away, I will spend every spare moment figuring out the meaning of "Audience." If I'm going to be a real writer, my audience will not be English teachers. It will be made up of many, many readers over my lifetime, including hundreds (thousands?) of people I've never met or even heard of, who will want to pay for my words. What a thought.

For the "project development" part, I'm going to write notes in my journal. I won't show Mr. Oliver my entire journal, of course: I will just copy and paste the useful bits into my assignment afterward. I might have a lot to say about this. Someone will actually read my writing! Who will that be? What will he/she think of me? I'm hoping that while I'm avoiding my grandmother, I'll write something brilliant. I don't mean "brilliant" in the sense that my parents' work is (according to the blurbs on the back of their books). My mom is working on *Geoffrey Chaucer, Feminism, and the Medieval Bodymind* (whatever *that* means). I love my mom, but I'd like to write something that NORMAL people read. Or any people, in fact.

So . . . about my tiny grandmother. She's nuts. Or, to use her own VERY English word, "bonkers." Tonight she was making pasta sauce in our kitchen, when she spotted a mosquito clinging to the wall above the cabinets. She hates mosquitoes. She made me get a chair so she could reach up and whack it. She grabbed the spoon she'd been using to stir the sauce, climbed up on the chair, and WHAMMO! The mosquito was three-dimensional one second and two the next.

She hadn't cleaned her weapon first, so when she whacked it, the pasta sauce went splattering halfway across the wall. It looked as though she had killed a small bird instead of an insect. Ed thought this was hilarious. And I had to clean it up, naturally. I did it in a hurry because I was VERY hungry by then, but mostly because I was afraid she'd turn off all the lights, grab a flashlight, and pretend to be on *CSI: Vancouver*. I'm not kidding. In my grandmother's world, life is one big comedy. Must be where my dad gets it from. I sure hope he can be serious when he gets to Oxford on this trip and has to eat dinners with somber academics in gowns.

But at least we didn't have to go to a yoga class for grannies. When she's at home in Seattle, she goes three times a week.

So far, she hasn't mentioned finding a class in Vancouver. I live in dread of being dragged along to sit cross-legged and chant with a bunch of old ladies.

At 6:00 PM on April 3, Thisbe said:
Hello everyone. Or, since I seem to be the only person here, "Hello, Me!" Right now, my grade for this project is an F. If anyone feels like posting something and raising it to an E, that would be great. In fact, I'd appreciate it so much that I'd make you a cinnamon bun. Just send me your email address, and I'll email it to you.

So you need more of an incentive? All right then. Since I know I'm not the only person with this site address, why don't I do a little dance to keep you shy folk entertained? *Bends down and laces on tap shoes. Coughs quietly and stands up, squinting into the bright lights.* Here we go.

Shuffle. Shuffle. Toe, heel, toe. Shuffle, stamp. Shuffle, ball change, stamp. TA-DA! Eyes and teeth! Sparkle!

I spoke to Mr. Oliver in the hallway at school today. He said it's ok if nobody else logs on to the blog. But that would be pointless! This whole assignment is about Audience, and I'll have to write for someone else—for real—sometime; someone other than my teacher, the Newly Bearded Wizard of Literature Land. He might give me marks for trying, but I'd be really disappointed, and I told him so, while trying not to stare at his facial hair. I think he would be, too. I think he had big ideas about bringing two schools together. Guess we aren't as willing as he thought. Guess he didn't realize How Wild The West still is, ha ha ha. Sounds like a bad cowboy movie starring Mr. Oliver as the hairy hero in huge pants and leather boots that look as though they've been chewed on and spat out.

Mr. Oliver paused for a moment, then said I would "still have to reflect on my experience." The reflections just have to be "authentic."

Well, NOBODY has replied yet, and it is making me authentically nervous. But now that I have spoken to Mr. Oliver, I must have earned at least 2.5% of that Project Development mark. Yippee.

When I told Melinda and Kel about my plans, they looked at me as if I had said the stupidest thing in the history of the world. Yet another moment when my famously sharp tongue fails me. There I was, ready to level some terrible insult—Kel was wearing that silly superior look she has (mainly because her vocabulary is so small, she probably used up all of her words earlier in the day)—and I think I said something like, "Oh sure, ok then." Killer.

Why is it that when I don't need to be nasty, I can make an incredibly witty observation that turns into a cutting put-down? That hurts someone's feelings. That ruins someone's day. That probably makes her go home and write about *me* in her journal. About how cruel I am. I didn't want to make a joke in the cafeteria about that blue-haired girl. I don't care if her hair is blue. And she doesn't really look like the girl who blows up into a massive blueberry in Willy Wonka's Chocolate Factory. She's not even slightly round, and if she were, why should I care? Why should I care if she puts stripes in her hair and lies in bed all day eating chocolate? It's not up to me what other people do. . . . I don't know why it seemed to matter before now. I don't want to think about the way her face looked after I made the Violet Beauregard comment.

But I do want to use my own writing for this project. I need to know what other people think of it. I thought my friends knew how important writing is to me. I guess I was wrong.

What will it be like if someone does respond? Will it be strange? Will it be fun? Will it be terrifying? Or jolly, thrilling, super, smashing, and terrific?

Note: These last words were included out of respect for my parents and the English relatives they are staying with. *Sorry.* With whom they are staying.

Wait. What if, after all these years, it's awful to have an audience? Maybe I am the only person who thinks my stories are any good? GULP.

RANDOM THOUGHT: Does nobody else my age want to be a novelist? What is wrong with them?

Well, let's see: Big surprise, Melinda and Kel are making an argument that classic novels should be turned into movies starring Jude Law and Ashton Kutcher. They're planning all of this on Kel's couch, eating popcorn and dreaming of their futures as movie stars. So meaningful. So Authentic. I can't wait for the sequel.

Mr. Oliver, by the way, is not a movie hero. He is not cool. I'm not cool. That's why we get along. I'm just a literature geek like my mom and dad. They quote Shakespeare when they burn the toast. Real world nothing. That's not why I write. If I wanted to be real, I'd log off and "socialize." Yeeuuch.

Nothing from Mom and Dad by email yet. Just a couple more phone calls that sound as though they've melted. Meanwhile, I am spending my nights with Granny Ed, watching TV while she scratches Chutney's head and shouts, "EAT SOMETHING!" at the women in my favorite shows. We were going to go out this evening, but after a fantastic sunny day, it suddenly started raining *really* heavily. Typical Vancouver. You think spring is here and then it pours—and you never know how long this miserable rain will stick around, if it's visiting or here for good. Kind of like Granny Ed and Chut.

WEDNESDAY

At 12:30 PM on April 4, Iphis said:
Hi Thisbe! Liked the dance. You might want to use your arms

more. ☺ Can I be part of your storytelling empire? What do I have to do? What is your plan, oh empress of the Web?

At 12:45 PM on April 4, Thisbe said:
Hey Iphis! Welcome to my empire. You have a weird name, too, I see. My subjects and I find this quite acceptable.

At 12:50 PM on April 4, Iphis said:
Yes, indeedy. This is the Kingdom of Strange Names. The Short Straws Club. How'd you get yours?

At 1:00 PM on April 4, Thisbe said:
I'm named after a character in a myth, via Shakespeare. It's about a girl who talks to her boyfriend through a hole in a wall . . . or something. Anyhow, I'm sure some terrible tragedy happened to this Thisbe character. My assignment certainly seems to be doomed. Three days in and NOTHING. BTW, most of my friends call me Fiz, so you may as well, too.

At 1:10 PM on April 4, Iphis said:
But of course. And you can call me Iphis. Er. *looks around expectantly* Who are your subjects?

At 1:11 PM on April 4, Thisbe said:
My words.

Ok, here's a bit about me. I'm in the computer lab right now. I go to Johnson High, as you know. I have a cat called Fishbone, which you probably don't. Fishbone looks really fat, but it's all fluff. He is a very chatty kitty. At the moment we talk mostly about hairballs (they are more of an issue for him, but there's a first time for everything . . . and I do have a lot of hair).

My parents aren't home now, but I'm not alone. Of course there is Fishbone and there is also my yoga-loving Granny Ed (that's short for Edna), who's staying here. Ed made me a "dessert" yesterday. It's still in the fridge. She thinks I can't cook, so she made this big tray of pastry flavored with tahini. Does this prove that she CAN cook? I don't think so. I don't eat meat. I love swimming.

At 1:14 PM on April 4, Iphis said:
Tahini? Animal, vegetable, or mineral?

At 1:16 PM on April 4, Thisbe said:
Hmm. Good question. Let me poke it and see if it moves.

At 1:21 PM on April 4, Iphis said:
Yum? I love desserts. It's handy because I must have a high metabolism. I never get fat (and I don't have Fishbone's excuse—it's not all fur!). I'm quite tall and on the *coughs* skinny side . . . and I'm at Westerley High (well, duh, obviously). Lunch break at the moment.

At 1:25 PM on April 4, Thisbe said:
Why is it called Westerley? I thought your school was on the east side of Vancouver?

At 1:26 PM on April 4, Iphis said:
It is. Westerley is some guy's name. :o)

At 1:26 PM on April 4, Thisbe said:

Ah, that explains it. Do I feel stupid now? Yep. Do you write? What do you write? *looks apologetic, as if auditioning brave newcomer; runs away and hides*

At 1:27 PM on April 4, Iphis said:

where'd she go? Yes, I write. Poems, mostly.

At 1:29 PM on April 4, Thisbe said:

returns, looking shy Can I see one?

At 1:31 PM on April 4, Iphis said:

Um . . . not yet. This is your world, Fiz. You do your stuff in here. I'll show you my poems later.

At 1:35 PM on April 4, Thisbe said:

Okeydokey, sounds good. ☺ And hey—I am short, by the way. Lab time's up! See you online tomorrow. . . .

Oh my gosh. Someone actually posted. She seems nice. She seems normal, i.e., slightly weird. And is she a *she*? Must be. I don't see any boys liking that dance. *This might actually work!* At least I have something to tell Mom and Dad. They finally hooked up the laptop at Uncle Al's in Oxford. Way better than the phone. The phone makes them sound as though they are on another planet (which may yet prove to be the case—for my dad, anyway). When I get email messages from them, I can pretend that they are emailing me from their offices at the university. It sounds as though they are having fun. First time they've been on a big trip like this without me. I don't mind, really. I think? I'm trying to be glad they're having their twentieth wedding anniversary trip and seeing all the people they miss from home. I mean *their* home. It's not my home. For me, trips to England have always been a vacation, just passing through, but seeing those people and those old places takes my parents right back to their childhood, or so they tell me. They sound really happy. They even get to have the trip paid for by their jobs because they are also doing research there. Or that's what they told the university. It's so they can write more "brilliant" books.

Granny Ed got me to write an email back saying hello, telling them about my class stuff, and describing all the wonderful meals we've had together. What do *they* know about food? They don't even cook with tahini . . . ha ha ha! We didn't talk about my p8ri8d (which started last month). I don't want to talk about it right now; that's why I haven't mentioned it before. Maybe that's what those sixteen phone calls from the airport were about? I hope Mom doesn't feel guilty about missing My Second Month As A Woman. I'd sure like to have missed it myself.

I was leaving school today, by myself, when a minivan drove past, really slowly. I glanced up at the people inside, who were climbing around. They were Melinda and Kel, crawling across the laps of the two boys in front (Golden Flirting Opportunity) to get to the backseats. The boys were older, of course—we can't drive yet. I recognized the one on the passenger's side as Lucas, the guy Melinda has been dating. He had grabbed a magazine (one of Melinda's?) and was flipping through the pages. As the minivan went by, he held up a page of the magazine to the car window. The girls were laughing so hard. I couldn't tell what was going on until I looked at the girl walking ahead of me. They were pointing at her, but she just kept on walking. She was a normal shape. A couple of sizes bigger than Melinda. So in other words, she hasn't been starving herself on sprouts and crackers for three weeks. She was probably going home to a great mom who makes sure that she eats a good meal before they go for a big walk together. She was healthy. She was fine. The girl in the magazine was the size of a knitting needle.

All of this happened in about two and a half seconds. Maybe the girl didn't even realize what was going on. I hope she didn't. At the traffic light, I caught up with the van and saw that Melinda and Kel were still howling with laughter. They were doubled up on the backseat, pretending to hide from the girl they'd been laughing at. They must have felt so cool, so in the in-crowd, so up-there. Huh. In a MINIVAN. Puh-leeaase . . .

As I was walking home, I felt really bad. It wasn't only on behalf of the other girl, either. Does that make me selfish? I hope not. I was thinking about my friends and what kind of person I must've been to have chosen them. It might have been in 2nd grade, but we must've had something in common then. When did Melinda and Kel and I become the kinds of people who laughed at other people like that? I can't believe I went along with it before. I could have made a different choice on any day. Does everyone else at school think I'm like them? I guess they do—and I can't blame them. But I hope people realize that I can think for myself and that I'm not just another member of the *ss-crack jeans crew. I don't want to use the B word, but my girls sure seem to be a couple of specimens. I feel as though I went for a space walk and before I knew it, I had cut my cord to the mother ship. I'm lost in outer space.

THURSDAY

Mr. Oliver asked me this morning how my project was coming along. I replied "great!" and thought *cha-ching*! One more percentage point. But really, I lied. One other person is talking to me. I still feel like I'm tap dancing in an empty theater, BUT Iphis does seem interesting. She writes poems. That's cool as long as they aren't epic poems. . . . I've had about as much epic as I can stand, having lived through the long and painful birth of my dad's book on *The Epic Poetry of John Milton: His Blindness and His Vision*. A blind man's visions, ha ha. . . . That has to be one of his worst puns. I don't think his editor even noticed, he was so preoccupied with the demons, angels, thunderbolts, and all that smiting stuff. Angels with wings. Sounds like they have their p8ri8ds.

At 10:10 AM on April 5, Iphis said:
Hey Thisbe the Frisbee! I am starting to feel comfy in here. I

brought my favorite chair along. Hope you don't mind. I'm pretty used to it, and it helps me do my best thinking. It's a bit shabby but we could cover it with a rug. . . .

At 10:10 AM on April 5, Thisbe said:
Of course you can bring a chair. But please DO NOT under any circumstances call me Frisbee.

At 10:11 AM on April 5, Iphis said:
looks sorry Oh. No problem.

At 10:12 AM on April 5, Thisbe said:
winks In any case, I am really The Chair-Person here, if you know what I mean. So let's see how this magically shabby chair helps you think! Let's see you get to work—kachaaah! *Thisbe cracks the whip then looks at it, wondering—oh, I have to write something first*

Are you comfy? Would you like a granola bar? I have some at the bottom of my book bag. They have been living under paperback books so they aren't too squished. Want some? I'll email them to you.

At 10:13 AM on April 5, Iphis said:
I might hold off for now. I have some cake crumbs and broken cookies here.

At 10:14 AM on April 5, Thisbe said:
Are you as addicted to your computer as I am? Does your computer

have a name? Come on, be honest now. Mine doesn't, but I have thought about it. Does that make me a geek? Would you rather email someone than phone them? Or see them? Are you capable of playing "just one game"?

At 10:15 AM on April 5, Iphis said:
topples under the weight of a million questions Addicted. Yes.

At 10:16 AM on April 5, Thisbe said:
I think (know) I eat more meals over my keyboard than the kitchen table. I could probably assemble an entire granola bar from the crumbs inside it. "Just one game?" Not a chance.

At 10:17 AM on April 5, Iphis said:
I love games—and Japanese animation! Hang on. I'm sending you the URL of my favorite game site. . . .

FRIDAY

At 10:10 AM on April 6, ANON said:
Hey! This is STUPID. My teacher told me I had to do it, so I am here and I won't be back. What's the point? This writing idea is dumb.

At 10:16 AM on April 6, Iphis said:
Dear Anonymous Author: You must have read something sometime because you seem to know about being "Anon." Otherwise you sound like a coward! Come out and show your face. We want to see you.

At 10:18 AM on April 6, Thisbe said:

Dear Iphis: Thank you for stepping in for me, but I think I will be ok. I can manage fine on my own. Anon is probably a Big Man and I am a Small Girl, but just watch me. . . .

At 10:20 AM on April 6, Thisbe said:

Hi Anon. While I appreciate your efforts to be witty, there is a fine line between giving someone a close shave and cutting their head off altogether. Let me spell it out for you. You have Crossed The Line. You will be deleted! I must ask you politely *smiles sarcastically* to curb your "enthusiasm" and stop showing off. We aren't interested. No arm wrestling, no sports-macho-look-at-me. Please show your intellectual prowess with elegant words in the future. Not your fists! Thank you. And now I'm going to leave this conversation up as a lesson to everyone else.

Signed, the elegant defender—Thisbe

At 10:22 AM on April 6, ANON said:

What are you going to do? MOOOOOUUUUWAHHAHAHAHA-HAH!!! You can't catch me!

At 10:26 AM on April 6, Iphis said:

Fiz . . . over to you?

Some idiot posted a message on Mr. Oliver's blog. I spoke to Mr. Oliver about it at lunch. He said he'd already seen the posting and that he'd get rid of it today. I'm picturing this in my mind. . . .

CUE: Cowboy music. *Nonny nonny nwooooargh . . .*

ENTER: The Cowboy Oliver, his new beard glinting. His pistol-sploosher is drawn. His eyes are narrowed against the brilliant sunshine and swirling dust.

The Cowboy Oliver's skin is burned dark brown by the beating rays. ANON quakes in his tiny boots. For an evil plot-meister, he has unusually small hands and feet. THWACK! The sploosher's work is done. ANON falls to the ground, completely immobilized but not dead, of course. The Cowboy Oliver never slays his enemies; he just puts their noses out of joint. He is, after all, a vegetarian. The cowering townsfolk pour out of their freshly squeezed juice bars and sushi stands [huh?], beaming with relief. The heroic cowboy simply touches the brim of his hat and swaggers toward his trusty steed, OSWALD. OSWALD and OLIVER ride off into the sunset, watched from a second-floor window by ANNA-LISA, the saloon-keeper's philatelist [I just learned that word today—nifty!] daughter. She is far too young for the cowboy, but that doesn't stop her from sighing over him. As he vanishes over the horizon, ANNA-LISA returns to the work of sorting stamps. She really likes the ones with fish on them. She is sure this means something.

At 12:34 PM on April 6, Thisbe said:
graciously accepts the floor from Iphis, cracking her whip To all of my faithful readers (sorry, *reader*) . . . it is with great regret that I must announce the passing of Anon. While his witticisms showed some intellectual promise, he strayed too

far into the darkness and recently found himself vanishing down the black hole that is Mr. Oliver's delete key. He might come back as someone else, but we trust that by then he will have learned the error of his ways. RIP Anon. Come back as YOURSELF, buddy.

At 12:35 PM on April 6, Iphis said:
Ha ha ha. I think we've all learned a valuable lesson today about allowing anonymous postings on our blogs, haven't we, class?

At 12:37 PM on April 6, Thisbe said:
winks at Iphis Hey, do you have IM?

At 12:41 PM on April 6, Iphis said:
Yes, but don't you think we should do this by email? It'll be easier to copy and paste later on.

At 12:43 PM on April 6, Thisbe said:
Good idea! I'll check with Mr. Oliver, but it should be fine as long as we don't share personal information, photos, etc.

At 12:43 PM on April 6, Iphis said:
Sounds good! Let's do it.

At 12:48 PM on April 6, Thisbe said:
Let's start new email addresses just for this assignment, ok? That should help us stay organized. I'll post my new address in just a sec. When I hear from you, I'll delete my posting. In the meantime, here's a random morsel for you: my favorite recipe. I usually make it with my mom, who does everything at a million miles an hour . . .

except when she's baking. Then she slows right down and can take four hours to make a single loaf of bread. I'll never understand this! My mom says baking is good because it forces her to have Brilliant Thoughts. I've tested out this theory but so far, the only thoughts I have are things like "I wonder if I could eat all of the buns in one sitting?"

Thisbe's Cinnamon Buns

3 1/4 cups plain flour
1 envelope quick-rise yeast
(2 1/4 tsp, I think)
1/4 cup sugar
1/2 tsp salt
3/4 cup milk
1/4 cup water
1/4 cup margarine
1 egg
1 cup brown sugar
1 tbsp cinnamon
1/2 cup margarine, softened
1/2 cup raisins—optional

Directions:

1. Mix flour (minus one cup), yeast, sugar, and salt in a bowl.
2. Heat the milk, water, and 1/4 cup margarine in a pan. When it's all hot and melty, add to dry stuff. Add the egg. Add a bit more flour until you get a dough that hangs together but isn't sticky. Take dough out of bowl and wallop it for a few minutes on a floured counter.
3. Next, make the yummy filling. Mix brown sugar, cinnamon, and 1/2 cup margarine together. Roll out the dough into a big rectangle and smear the goop all over it. Throw in raisins if you like them. Roll up the whole thing and lean on the ends, so the filling doesn't fall out.
4. Cut into 12 slices. Squeeze slices into a 12-cup muffin pan

(don't forget to grease it first). Leave pan somewhere warm for 20 minutes. Bake at 375 until the buns are brown and/or the smell drives you crazy and you can't wait any longer. Eat cinnamon bun warm with tall glass of milk. Eat remaining 11 buns in one go. When you have finished licking the sugary goop off your fingers, send Thisbe a thank you note.

I was in a really bad mood tonight. So bad that when Granny Ed tried to talk me out of it, I snapped at her. She was surprised. And all I could do was stare at her. I felt SO mean. People my age don't stick around when you're mean. They just go away. It's as if I had swallowed whatever potion it is that makes Melinda and Kel so nasty to people these days. Like the girl in the cafeteria with the blue hair. They've given her a hard time ever since I made that joke about Extreme Adventures With Blueberries. I've regretted it ever since.

You know, Melinda's been a good friend, but now she is completely wrapped up in her boyfriend, Lucas. She's like a carrot in a Ziploc bag. She can't breathe but she doesn't know it—and not just because they were trying to swallow each other outside our math class this afternoon. Kel is obsessed with finding a boyfriend now that Melinda has one.

Wait. The phone's ringing.
It was Kel. So I guess she has found one. Minivan Boy #2 is now "Rob." There goes another friend. I guess you could say . . . I've been "Robbed."

Anyhow, Granny Ed was trying again (poor her—I should come with a warning label) to help me feel better about the whole p8ri8d thing. Mom told her. I said I had practically given up on swimming and that I hated my body. That I wanted to climb out of it, wanted to be a cloud . . . bodyless, shapeless, formless, amorphous like thc lovely amoeba. This is a very big deal because the outdoor pools open soon and I'm usually there on Day 1. Gran told me that I was "out of touch with my body" and took my hand. I pulled my hand away and said, "Out of touch? Too bad—I'll send it an email."

She wasn't much impressed with that. And to tell the truth, neither was I. I went upstairs and buried my face in Fishbone's fur. That's one thing that always makes me feel better. Fishy is so in touch with *his* body.

SATURDAY

From: Thisbe
To: Iphis
Subject: Audience participation

Is audience participation really allowed in this thing, do you think? If I change my stories because of something you've said, is that still ok? Is it still "my" story? Where do we draw the line? Let me tell you why I'm asking: it is so *unbelievably* hard to write something all in one go, all on your own. I had the idea that I would write a big chunk to share with you, and then we'd take that chunk, your response, and our emails and make something of it. Bingo! Instant assignment.

But now I'm worried. I can't just write from the beginning to the end. It's not like running a race, with a definite start and a finish line. What if I *need* you to help me finish something? Would we still say I'd written it? I have sat at my computer for hours this week. Nothing. Nothing, nothing, nothing . . . (except my journal) (which nobody wants to read)(and which I wouldn't share with you, anyway)? *breaks into a sweat at the very thought of it* What am I going to do?

Signed, the queen of parentheses and ellipses

From: Iphis
To: Thisbe
Subject: Re: Audience participation
Dear Queen of the Paren-Thisbes—I think it's supposed to be like falling off a log. You can do it. You can. Just close your eyes and fall. I'll be here to catch you, I promise! Just start typing and see what comes out of your fingers.

From: Thisbe
To: Iphis
Subject: *peers at her fingers*
Like a hangnail? I am very worried that my mind can't handle the beginning-to-end thing. I've written a ton of stories, but when I go back to read them, they are either (a) not finished or (b) only finished in my head. Which basically means they aren't even *started*. . . . Whoops. And I'm nervous about telling Mr. Oliver that I can't do it—I must have seemed so confident. I just knew that I couldn't do what the rest of the class is doing. Since it's a "collaborative" project, everyone picked their friends. I didn't want to work with my friends this time. In fact, I don't

even know if they are my friends???

BUT enough of my rambling. Falling off a log (in fact, from the top of a large cedar) would be easier right now. So here goes. Don't stare in case I scrape my knee, ok?

From: Iphis
To: Thisbe
Subject: Re: *peers at her fingers*
Ten-four. Have fun logging off! You can do it. Careful as you go. . . .

SUNDAY

Tonight Granny Ed had to go and check on her friend Norm. I thought maybe it was a date, but she said no—he's sick. She gave me a long stare. Probably thinking (quite rightly) that my dad is suspicious of her friendship with Norm. My dad doesn't really like the idea of her seeing Norm, but I think it's ok. They were all friends, for a long time, before Grandpa Michael died. And it's been two years. I think it's ok if she sees him (or even *sees* him?).

So I'm on my own with Chutney and Fishbone, until she gets home later. I don't want to watch TV so I'm curled up on the couch, around Fishbone, with my laptop. I talked to him until he got bored or changed the subject, and then I read Mom and Dad's emails again. Dad says jetlag has turned him into one of the seven dwarves on each day of their trip so far. On the first day, it made him Sleepy, then Dopey, and then Grumpy. But then I realized: my dad's pretty much like a cartoon character even when he ISN'T jetlagged. . . .

Chutney just wandered off into the kitchen. I've kept a close eye on him, to make sure he doesn't stray into Cat Zone. . . . So far so good. Fishbone has one eye open and is looking at me with what Gran calls his "sneer of cold command." She says it with a flourish so I know it's a quote. Man, this family has quotes coming out of their EARS. Why do they always have to quote *someone else*?

I need another dose of Mom-medicine. I miss her. If she were here now, we'd be sending Dad out for a tennis game. Mom and I have good nights at home, when he's not here— not like before. I used to ignore her. But now, when he's working late or playing tennis, we talk to each other. It used to be—we had to be doing something. Always busy, that's Mom. She's moving, moving, always moving. Dad says she has two gears: stop and go. And sometimes he compares her to a train. He says she speeds into dark landscapes all the time. He must love her so much to think up descriptions like that. And the train thing sounds like me, too. He hardly speaks to me these days, but maybe I don't talk to him much, either, since Grandpa Michael died. . . . I don't know.

Wow. I'm really rambling. Rambling like a blackberry bramble, wild and thorny and free! Ha ha ha, listen to me. I must be tired or confused or something. Fishy was right. I'm not making much sense.

I did something so stupid tonight. I can't tell Mom or Dad or they will never take another vacation. Disaster! I am almost afraid to tell Granny Ed, but I must remember (a) what a nutcase she is and (b) how she never thinks anything is actually a PROBLEM. Somehow everything is just a big joke to her. Breathe. Breathe.

Ok. So here's what happened: I have the dishwasher all neatly filled, with the plates in the right place and the glasses in the upper drawer so they don't rattle. Following my mother's Very Serious Rules For Loading Dishwashers, which my dad struggles with every time. I am so certain I've done it perfectly. But I still have to add the detergent. So I reach into the cabinet under the sink and pull out a big yellow bottle. Glug, glug, gloop. In it goes, on goes the dishwasher, and I go upstairs to do my homework. Fishbone is already upstairs, of course, keeping that spot on my bed warm (just in case I feel the urgent need to sleep on that very spot myself; he's considerate that way).

Half an hour later, while Granny Ed is busy taking care of Norm and I'm busy being very responsible and mature all by myself, I go downstairs to get a glass of milk. What do I hear? The dishwasher?! In the throes of some awful disease. Or anguish. Or terror. At any rate, it's groaning horribly, and I'm fairly certain it's not washing dishes. It doesn't even sound as though there's any water in there.

But how can that be? I followed the Very Serious, Etc. Rules to a T! Religiously! I approach the groaning beast and open the door very cautiously. What do I see? No water. Not a drop in sight, but a mountain and a FLOOD of bubbles. The entire dishwasher is foam, foam, more foam, foam as far as the eye can see, creeping up on me, dripping over the sides of the dishwasher door and onto my favorite pair of slippers. Foam, crawling across the kitchen floor, ready to swallow the table and chairs and poor, unsuspecting, loyal Fishbone, who has followed me down into the kitchen.

For a moment I just stare. Those must have been the groans of death. I've broken the dishwasher. But how??? I'm in a state of total panic. Then I look at the big yellow bottle of . . . **OH NO!** . . . dish soap. I grabbed the wrong bottle. I read the label: "For hand washing only. Not to be used in dishwashers." How dumb could I be? Very?

As the foam rises and I scoop Fishy into my arms, my mind races. What do dishwashers cost? More than my allowance for a whole year? I have no idea! Can I replace this one with an exact copy, dent the bottom right-hand side with my book bag, and peel the label off just the right way, so my parents don't notice that it's a different machine?

But my math assignment is due tomorrow, and it could take me another seven hours to finish it. So I do the responsible, mature thing and close the dishwasher door until it clicks. Then I put Fishy down, check that he floats, and set about cleaning the kitchen floor. I've just poured more soap on it than it's seen in years, so by the time I'm done, it's sparkling like in a TV commercial. GREAT! When Granny comes home, I'll just pretend that I was filled with the urge to wash the kitchen floor. She'll never guess the truth. That is, until she opens the dishwasher and instantly finds herself neck-deep in lemon-fresh foam. *I have to tell her.*

Must be time to go to bed. Come on, Fiz, do the right thing. Lights out, girl. SIGH. Will call Mom tomorrow with calling card. Ssshhh. . . . Now, go to bed. Don't—Think—About—The—Dishwasher.

Zzz . . .

Week Two, April 9

MONDAY

I did call Mom before school. It was mid-afternoon for them, so they were having tea. I feel better. I feel as though I can do this. Didn't talk to Dad for too long, but it was still good to hear his voice. He and Uncle Al were laughing hysterically in the next room for most of the call. I could hear Al doing that funny snorting thing he does when he laughs too hard. Mom said it was weird being surrounded by English people. Mom and Dad are so used to hearing Canadians all the time, now Brits are the ones with the accents. I guess they don't hear their own voices much. Mom said everything seems smaller than she remembered, the sky is gray, and the traffic is terrible. She is, however, "feasting her eyes" on things that seem both familiar and strange. I can't imagine what that must be like.

And did I mention the Dishwasher Disaster to them? What? Do you think I'm stupid?

I got a pointless French exam back today. I was so sure I'd failed. Getting 84% was such a huge relief. I don't know why I was worried, though—my dad wouldn't care about my failing. He'd think it was funny. Just as he was leaving for England, he emailed me from his office downstairs, reminding me to "send your father breaking news of all your glorious school successes!!!" He wasn't serious. Not at all. My parents don't care about grades. This must be the one thing my father has in common with Granny Ed. It's pretty ironic, really. For someone who cares so little about grades, he's been in school a long time. Maybe it's different if you're on the other side of the teacher's desk??

My dad took years to finish his PhD and become a professor. When I was little, Grandpa Michael used to tease my dad about choosing the name "Thisbe" for me. Grandpa said it had nothing to do with Shakespeare or any old myths. He said it was short for "Will your THesIS BE finished soon?"

Bizarre. I am NOT like my dad. I can't wait to finish school.

Ow. Argh. Dishwasher. Argh, etc.

Dishwasher Disaster: BREAKING (that's not a pun) NEWS!
PHEW. Granny Ed has saved my skin. She has saved my savings, too. . . . There I was, convinced I'd be blowing it all on a new dishwasher for my poor parents, when Granny Ed came back from walking Chutney (I must pause to hold my nose. That dog smells like . . . a dog). I told her that we should find out what kind of religious ritual applies to the passing of dishwashers. Burial? Cremation? Whom or what do dishwashers worship?

So while I was thinking these Deep Spiritual Thoughts, Granny just hustled Chut under the kitchen table with his stinky treat and said, "oh, nonsense!" in that sensible way she has. I love it when she becomes all practical like that. I couldn't believe what she did next. She didn't empty the dishwasher. And she didn't start bailing out the foam with a bucket. I was already anticipating her awful sailing-on-the-high-seas jokes with every bucket she filled . . . but no.

She just reached into the evil cabinet under the sink (evil because it casts spells on the DISH SOAP and makes young girls think it is dishwasher detergent) and grabbed a couple of little sponges. She tossed them both into the dishwasher and set the machine going again. Boy do I feel even more stupid. That's all it took. An hour later, after some quality television time, the machine stopped gurgling and there it was: sparkly plates and not a bubble in sight. Thank goddess for grandmothers. She surely saved my butt.

TUESDAY
From: Thisbe
To: Iphis
Subject: *hands Iphis the microphone*
So what's *your* thing (please tell me it's not YOGA)? You know all about my writing obsession.

From: Iphis
To: Thisbe
Subject: Re: *hands Iphis the microphone*
looks eager and excited I like basketball. I LOVE anime. I taught myself to draw the people . . . you know, with big hair and unusually long legs.

From: Thisbe
To: Iphis
Subject: clumpy hair
Oh yes—I know the kind you mean. I'd love to see your drawings, too! You must be a great artist. I know I am. . . . It's just that whenever I pick up a pencil and try to draw, the pencil refuses to bow to my artistic genius and insists on producing stick figures.☺

From: Iphis
To: Thisbe
Subject: *looks angrily at Thisbe's naughty pencils*
How frustrating! You should read those labels carefully. I only buy the passive kind. Let me talk to my army of pencils and see what they can produce for you.

From: Thisbe
To: Iphis
Subject: *looks hopeful*
You are a most generous commander! I bless you and your army of gentle pencils. May your next campaign bring exciting (artistic) adventures, vast new territories (of paper), and a multitude of loyal new subjects (to draw)!

From: Iphis
To: Thisbe
Subject: *waving graciously from a white marble balcony*
Many benedictions to you likewise, your empress-ness! And now I offer my royal farewell because it's time to GET TO WORK, CHICKIE! I WANT TO SEE SOME REAL WRITING! *pauses to cough—not used to shouting*

From: Thisbe
To: Iphis
Subject: *recovers from extraordinary volume of Iphis's command*
Ok. Don't judge. *she speaks in a tiny, tiny, small voice* How it is, is how it is. Will write from the top of my head, the bottom of my heart, and the ends of my fingers. Here I go. Free fall. Timberrrr . . . !

From: Iphis
To: Thisbe
Subject: *looks attentive and sprouts a few extra ears*
Ready and waiting. All ears.

From: Thisbe
To: Iphis
Subject: that sure is a lot of ears
Ha ha, Lady-in-Waiting.
My name is Thisbe. I have always known that I want to be an author. There is no other choice, but guidance counselors hate me for it. They want to tell me which course to take, but they never tell me to go into creative writing. They're probably afraid that they'd lose their jobs for depriving the world of another lawyer/doctor/ accountant. Thou Shalt Go To College and Thou Shalt Join The Knowledge Economy! My way of joining the global info-glut super-knowledge economy is to become a novelist. Sounds unlikely, but it's true. In just the same way that I despise prepackaged sauces, I've known since I was six that I couldn't digest other people's words forever. I have to find (or make?) some of my own.

From: Iphis
To: Thisbe

Subject: Re: that sure is a lot of ears

Nice metaphors, chickie—but I think you actually have to write a story. Or were you getting to that? I was thinking I'd do my reader's response thing in between bits of story. Just a thought. Thanks for sharing your lifelong ambition, too. I don't have one.

From: Thisbe
To: Iphis
Subject: all ears

I'm panicking. What was I thinking? But ok. I will log off now (or do I mean, fall off?) and see what Fishbone thinks. He usually has some good ideas. More soon. Ambition: you will find one.

From: Iphis
To: Thisbe
Subject: no problem

Good luck. I'll do my homework until you email me. Ambition: Does basketball count? Does making the world record for eating blueberry waffles count? What about being able to watch four anime DVDs back-to-back?

Guess what? Granny Ed is a vegetarian, just like me. I realized it only this week. The other day, she came back with leftovers from her visit to Norm. Having eaten the food she brought back, I've decided that my dad should *definitely* stop being suspicious of Ed's friends. Norm gave her directions to make dinner. It was a vegetarian noodle dish. Delicious! I slurped the last few noodles down (yum, carbohydrates).

I just can't eat animal parts these days, either. It wasn't always that way. I used to eat chicken and beef like everyone else. Or like my parents, at least. But now the smell of meat cooking makes me feel ill. And the look of it on a plate! Ugh. I can't stand it. My dad thinks my being a vegetarian is very cute and funny. He says it's just a phase, but I don't think so. How can you eat something that used to be alive? What if it had a name? It seems that Granny Ed agrees with me. It's strange that I didn't think of that before. Maybe that's why my dad loves his roasts so much. He must have hated growing up in Ed's house! Look how he rebelled. Wow, she must have been shocked when he shaved, wore corduroys, and knitted his own vests. What, no beard? No yoga? No sandals? No tie-dyed shirts?! Eeek! The rebellious, meat-eating man with the veggie hippie mom. And maybe that's why I am not an omnivore. No meat for rebel Thisbe.

Anyhow. Can't write more. Changed the picture on my screen a few times. Have been through my entire stock of last year's road-trip photos. Might start on the folder of Fishbone photos next.

WEDNESDAY

Just pulled out the shoe box with my old journals in it. . . . I can't really remember a time when I didn't write. I wonder if I started just because my parents were always writing, and I was trying to fit in.

When I read over my journals, they seem so sad. When it's

not about the Cowboy Oliver, of course. It all seems to be one long complaint—especially since Grandpa Michael died and my dad stopped talking to Granny Ed. Or rather, he didn't stop talking to her. As my mom says, he just needed some time to "lick his wounds." It wasn't Grandpa dying that wounded him the most, I think. It was not being told Grandpa was sick until so late. By the time we found out, Grandpa was already pretty weak. . . . We were all so shocked. He seemed so young. So strong. And then all of a sudden, he was gone. Maybe that was when the Era of Weird really started. Sometimes I forget he's gone. But I shouldn't be angry with Gran—not really. Kids are always left out of the loop. Especially when it's something important. But of course, it's one thing to know this and another thing to be as mature and sensible as I'm supposed to be.

And now Granny Ed is alone. Or not quite alone. I guess she has Chutney—who my father named, and it stuck (he had a good snort over that, "because Chutney is *very* sticky, isn't it?!" Ha ha, very funny, Dad). But at least Granny seems happier since she got Chut. We actually talk to her now, and my dad doesn't huff and puff about it so much.

I am beginning to feel better about losing Grandpa Michael. Even though he was the best friend I had, outside my little group of girls . . . On my list of "10 Things I Love" he came up under:
• Grandpa Michael's apple pancakes AND
• Walking on the beach with Grandpa Michael, bringing home silty, salty, silly things that my mom wanted to put in

the dishwasher before they could go in my box of treasures, but I wouldn't let her.

So I've lost two things from my list. I'm down to eight, and the other eight weren't anything to shout about.

Maybe I should take my journals and turn them into papier-mâché or just paint over them. Maybe paintbrushes wouldn't mutiny when I pick them up. I can show 'em who's boss. (Or maybe I can learn not to care that my art is terrible . . . ?) I don't want my journal to be a place for sadness. Once something is written down, it feels permanent. It's like wallowing in failures and friendships that have gone sour, and disappointments of all shapes and sizes. There have been a few of those lately. Melinda and Kel, what are they thinking? Our old group feels like a club I don't belong to anymore. I'm just the hanger-on-er, following them around.

I think this journal should be a place to rehearse my victories. What if I told only the story I wanted to tell? Retell my life story like it's one of my own stories . . . except that I wouldn't know how it ends! I can tell a story about being a wicked success. It's my journal, after all. This is where I should be the person I wish I were. I could persuade myself, make it permanent in words, and then I really *will* change.

There's a huge gap between the person I see through the cracks between my fingers and the person I ought to be. I know that now. I am not as nice as I should be. My "friends" (so-called, slobbing at Kel's house tonight in front of endless reruns) don't help. They always laugh when I make jokes about other people. And it encourages me! Which is foolish because the spears are only an excuse for the sharp things that point inward. Those do a lot more damage. Like regrets about the girl with blue hair. I can't believe I was so mean to her.

THURSDAY

From: Thisbe
To: Iphis
Subject: no problem

I feel a story coming. 'Tis in the works. . . .

Characters are swimming in and out of my head. There is a family called Jones. Yesterday the Jones family had no neighbors for miles, and Jeremy Jones had no siblings. Today he has a much younger sister (mysterious, huh?) with blond ringlets and captivating green eyes. Her name is Robin, and many of the neighbors think this name is a strange choice. No, Robin is not there. She is actually a neighbor's daughter with whom the Jones boy is strangely fascinated. The younger Jones, that is. Trevor. He thinks she looks like an angel of the prairies. No, wait—cornfields. It is Saskatchewan, 1935.

Robin inspires Trevor to work harder, to repaint the side of the shed that faces her parents' property. He's working away on a pile of hay in the middle of his father's field. He drops his pitchfork into the hay bale and gazes into the cloudless azure sky. He wonders if he dares leave his parents' modest property so that he may travel, see the city, and return worldly enough to prove himself to Robin.

He has barely spoken to her, but he has seen how she never leaves the house without her hat and a book, even if she has no shoes. It's not always the same book, either. She could tell him what was in each one. Maybe it's poetry. Trevor is almost sure it's poetry. The romantic kind.

What Trevor doesn't know is that Robin is, in fact, reading a tractor manual and has no intention of being swept off her dirty feet by a man with big, hairy hands; no education; and only just enough money for a train ticket. She, at the ripe age of thirteen (and she sure looks ripe to Trevor), is determined to understand how the combustion engine works. She wants to know how the Statue of Liberty reached New York and in how many pieces. She wants to understand why her father's harvester is "a piece of worthless cr✳p," as he calls it, and she's going to the university to become an engineer. She might meet a man there. She might meet several men. But no matter what, she won't be living here a minute longer than she has to. One thing is certain: Trevor and the three other farmhands like him are not her cup of tea. Or other hot beverage.

Author's note: I'm a bit worried about this story. I don't really know anything about farming. Or cornfields. Or 1935.

From: Iphis
To: Thisbe
Subject: Re: no problem
Why should it matter? Just make it up. That's why it's called *fiction*. . . . *backs up* But seriously: nice start! Love the

imagery . . . pitchforks, hay bales. Are you into sexual imagery or what? Yowzer.

From: Thisbe
To: Iphis
Subject: ". . . . ."
What?

From: Iphis
To: Thisbe
Subject: Re: ". . . . ."
"What" is right. You have you-know-what on the brain.

From: Thisbe
To: Iphis
Subject: Re: Re: ". . . . ."
PAH. *Thisbe utters this with complete nonchalance. She is disdainful that Iphis would even imagine that impure thoughts could enter her youthful mind*

From: Iphis
To: Thisbe
Subject: Re: Re: Re: ". . . . ."
Denial is a muddy river.

From: Thisbe
To: Iphis
Subject: of course not!
Denial? What, ME? Not a chance.
Stand by! I'm changing the subject.

I have survived another evening with Granny Ed's dog. The creature is small but takes up a LOT of room. He is called Chutney, and he is SO neurotic. Always bouncing and getting excited to see Gran. Very inelegant. Very gross. And very un-Fishbone-like. Fishy is the picture of grace. I'm sure it has something to do with names. Fishhhhhhy just rolls off the tongue . . . smooooothly. . . . But Chutney??? My dad says there is a lesson here. "If you want your pet to be well-balanced, do not name him after a condiment." He should know. The name is HIS fault.

From: Iphis
To: Thisbe
Subject: pet names (not that kind of pet name, silly!)
You might have a point. Maybe I shouldn't get a fish and call it Tartar, ha ha ha.

From: Thisbe
To: Iphis
Subject: saucy pet names
Ha ha ha ha ha. By the way, I hate to think what else we might have called Fishbone. With his extra toes, I'm not sure he's really part of any species. Especially "cat."

From: Iphis
To: Thisbe
Subject: toes???
Extra toes? Scary. Explain before story, please.

From: Thisbe
To: Iphis
Subject: Re: toes???

Yes, it's the awful truth. We went to the rescue place about five years ago to get a kitten, and my parents fell on Fishy with great yelps, as if they'd met an old friend. Fishbone has six toes on each foot. So did some author's many cats. Was it Hemingway? I can never keep these things straight. So they probably thought Fishbone would inspire them to write the next great, dark, twisted work of critical literary thingummy. . . . Course, at that age, I was hoping to get a pet that reminded me of a dainty tutu-wearing BALLERINA, but no. . . . We got a cat that is, quite possibly, no relation to some dead, famous author's pets. If I even have that part right.

From: Iphis
To: Thisbe
Subject: Re: Re: toes???

That's hardcore pet tragedy, friend. But I bet he kicks butt at handball. . . . And now . . . a story if you please?

From: Thisbe
To: Iphis
Subject: A what? Oh yes . . .

stretches, yawns, and prepares to fire up some new brain cells
Sure. ☺

FRIDAY

Iphis is encouraging me to write, but it's really hard to focus. And not just because it's getting warm outside. Or because I nearly blew up the dishwasher.

You can't just sit down and write if the story hasn't come to you yet. I like the way that people say a story "unfolds." It's so true. You find it in a little corner of your brain all folded up like a tiny origami animal; then as you stay with it, it unravels itself and you start to see a bigger picture. Characters and settings and dialogues and feelings all fall out of the folds. Writing is like being lost in a labyrinth, where you are running down all those wrong ways and dead ends . . . until you find the exit and are free, quite by accident. I know that I have my metaphors mixed and my mother would be furious, but hey, I deserve a break. Don't I? At least I am writing about writing.

You write, you write, you change your mind, someone else changes your mind (you have to know your mind in the first place, of course). You say NO! Not Vancouver, New York! No rainforest clouds and rocky shorelines. A city with skyscrapers and traffic and people everywhere. It's 1862. No, it's 1975. No. Wait. I wasn't even alive in 1975, either. 2002. Wait. There's no house. Let me build one. It's a white house with steps that go up between two black railings, and . . .

Our presentation will be due soon. What will I say? I really expected to get a finished story out of this Audience assignment; but what if I don't? Maybe my title for this thing should be "Why you can't write a novel in twelve weeks." Mr. Oliver told me another group is working on the blog now, but they wisely are sticking to books written by *other* people.

And I think this icky feeling in my stomach means I am missing my mom and dad. Even if Dad does still wear those terrible corduroys. I wish he wouldn't. They make him look like Grandpa, when he *isn't* Grandpa. Maybe the icky feeling in my stomach means I am really missing Grandpa. It still feels so recent. I don't understand how Granny Ed can be so fine. Maybe she isn't fine, but she seems to be doing better than I am—on the outside, at any rate.

I tried to be so "mature," telling my parents to take this trip. I tried to be unselfish, tried to put them first, but every day with Granny Ed just makes me think more and more of Grandpa. Hmm. Come to think of it, maybe that's why they went away and left me with her. Make me "come to terms with my loss," etc. etc. etc. . . . . Seems like my selflessly mature thing really backfired this time. For it to work, I think you actually have to BE selfless and mature. It was a good theory, but since I can't pull it off, I'm a bit of a mess. I can't finish my project. I can hardly start it. I just look at Chutney, sitting under Granny Ed's chair, and see the empty spot next to her, where Grandpa used to sit.

Just read over my last few journal entries. Have decided that I am obsessed with myself. This Is Not Good. Not Good At All. It's weird and pathetic, in fact. Will try not to be so obsessed in the future.

It's annoying, though, that one day the girls act as if I don't exist; the next day they're like my best friends again. Oh, these stupid cat-and-mouse games (no offense, Fishbone!). I'll never understand these people. It feels as though I've lost my immunity, failed on a challenge, been voted off the island—or whatever this week's reality show is. But the important thing is this: I must leave no evidence of these dangerous thoughts! The very thought of Melinda seeing them is enough to make me perspire in a very unladylike fashion. Which is next to criminal, since I am now a Young Lady.

I know! I'll tackle my journal instead of my actual life. Tackle the fiction version of it, anyway. I have a great idea.

THE END

Ok, so it's nowhere near the end. The end of what? I just thought it would be cool to type THE END and see what it was like. Rehearsal number one. Now I just need to write the 199 pages that come first.

Why do I feel so much pressure to get my Audience project done? Mr. Oliver feels no pressure. He has had my poetry assignment for three weeks. The pile of papers on his desk is growing by the day with no grade in sight. It's almost a hill. By next week it's sure to be a mountain.

COWBOY OLIVER gazes at the mountain (not of cactus- and scrub-covered landscape, but of student papers). His trusty horse, OSWALD, is flicking his tail at the flies, feeling thirsty. COWBOY OLIVER contemplates the mountain for the hundredth time and decides not to scale its forbidding slopes. He turns his back, and OSWALD'S bottom, toward the mountain and slowly ambles back to town, where the hospitality of the ever-adoring saloon-keeper's daughter, ANNA-LISA, and her famous vegetarian chili await them (OSWALD is rather partial to her chili, too—it's not just for cowboys). ANNA-LISA has finished sorting a new shipment of fish stamps and is thinking of branching out into reptiles. Or maybe birds?

No, she thinks. Birds are too girlie. Snakes it is.

SATURDAY

From: Iphis
To: Thisbe
Subject: you can do it

You are REALLY SMART, Fiz. Maybe you should stop writing and start reading. You have some good stuff here! That Robin story was great. Why not read it a few times and see if it sparks off some new ideas? Or . . . want to see some of mine? I have a poem that I can't finish. Would like your input. Not for the assignment or anything.

From: Thisbe
To: Iphis
Subject: so can you

Sure. Fly at it.

From: Iphis
To: Thisbe
Subject: but can I?

takes deep breath Ok. Here goes. Will try to be brave, like you.

<u>Leavings</u>
Love is not like glue.
It cannot stick people together
Because you want it to.
You might think this is all,
This is my world and what there is—
But nothing is forever.
I might love you and you might
Love me, but we are unglued, unstuck.

We have no time, you've gone
With her. I'm out of luck. I miss
Our nights in, the conversations
We had—

That's where I can't finish it. I think it's because my feelings aren't finished yet.

From: Thisbe
To: Iphis
Subject: Re: but can I?
It's so good, Iphis. It's definitely going somewhere. I don't know where yet, but the feeling is so genuine, and that is the first step, I think? Sorry . . . you sound really heartbroken. *fidgets, wishing she could do something* Should I distract you?

From: Iphis
To: Thisbe
Subject: Re: Re: but can I?
Sure, give it your best shot. What are you going to do? Another dance? Thanks for the feedback, by the way—I haven't shown that poem to anyone else yet.

From: Thisbe
To: Iphis
Subject: another story
Thank you for trusting me.
And no, it's not a dance. . . . It's the ending to "The Tragedy of Trevor and Robin" (although it's only really a tragedy if you are Trevor) (and by the way? He's not called Trevor anymore. His name is

Elijah. Elijah Sprout. Which makes this "The Tragedy of Elijah Sprout." Has a certain ring to it, dontchathink?).

pause to reveal dastardly secret I get my characters' names from a special email address I set up, just for junk mail. I get TONS of spam in it, and it's always from people with crazy names. But it's not as though I'm stealing anyone's identity—none of those people are real, right?

From: Iphis
To: Thisbe
Subject: Re: another story
I'm liking this. I am distracted. *wipes eyes, blows nose loudly*
And no, I don't think it's identity theft. There cannot possibly be that many people called "Dolores" in the world.

From: Thisbe
To: Iphis
Subject: Re: Re: another story
ducks to avoid flying hankie Ha ha ha, I'm going to start calling YOU Dolores.
But ok: I'm putting my storytelling hat on.

SIX YEARS LATER
Robin has come home from the university where she has been working hard to become an engineer, and working just as hard to avoid the fleshpots of Toronto (New York?) and to beat boys at chess. A brilliant strategist, she has learned that her blond curls are extremely diverting to young men. She makes a tidy profit from her chess games during evenings and weekends.

From: Iphis
To: Thisbe
Subject: Re: Re: Re: another story
Does she have a cape, a mask, and a secret life yet?

From: Thisbe
To: Iphis
Subject: the continuing tragedy of Elijah Sprout
SSshhhh! Art thou my worshipping Audience or art thou not? I just hit SEND to get the Audience assignment thingy in gear. Right. As I thought . . .

Robin returns to the farm in the summer to help her parents. She is back for only a few weeks, but that is enough time for Elijah, as he watches her daily trips out into the fields from his kitchen window. The flames of his passion burn brightly in short, flickering, painful bursts. His heart pounds as she marches purposefully toward her father's combine with a wrench in one hand and a book in the other. She is now nineteen, and she still wears no shoes. Elijah watches her hair blowing gently in the breeze, sees the orange morning light on her face, and moves his hands around the pot he is scrubbing, slowly, slowly, in circular motions. There she goes.

From: Iphis
To: Thisbe
Subject: Re: the continuing tragedy of Elijah Sprout
Loving her from a distance, eh? Sounds like the thing for you. NOTE TO THISBE: The suspense is killing me. Does he go after her?

From: Thisbe
To: Iphis
Subject: the continuing tragedy . . .
Glad you're on the edge of your seat—because I'm not finished!
Although I'm not sure about sending this to my teacher. Gulp. I'm
pretty careful about who sees my writing. Don't forget, you have to
be my Audience here, as well as my friend. The presentation part
is coming up soon, so I have to have something to report. How
about we don't let Mr. Oliver know you're my buddy, ok? This is
supposed to be work. *Gives the stern-taskmaster look to Iphis,
who is doodling in the margins of her book. Iphis looks up
sheepishly, grins, and grabs her clipboard and glasses* And by the
way, I'm going to use the past tense from now on for this story. I
don't think novels happen in the present tense. Oops.

From: Iphis
To: Thisbe
Subject: getting tense?
Sounds good. Keep going.

From: Thisbe
To: Iphis
Subject: getting tense
As she walked away from him, Elijah began to feel anxious. It wasn't
the actual distance between his sink and her vanishing back.
Something important was missing. She had no shoes, but that
was normal for her during the summer. Suddenly it dawned on
him. With a twisting in his stomach, Elijah realized that Robin had
embarked on a hot day's work without food or drink. She would be
working in a field that was miles from home.

Elijah put down his pot and set to work. He hurried into his pantry. He sliced off huge pieces of bread and hunks of cheese, which he wrapped carefully in wax paper. He found two crisp green apples and filled a tin bottle with water, right to the brim. He reached into every box and shelf until he found just the right combination of delicious morsels. There could be no doubt about this meal. It would tell her everything she needed to know about him. No corner of her stomach would be left empty. She would know the extraordinary depth of his passion. His love was written in every morsel and drop and every fold of the wax paper in which her noonday meal was wrapped.

All of those summers of stolen gazes, of watching Robin grow from a child to a young adult to a confident, determined woman. It had all come to this. Every tiny moment, every breath, every day and night had led to now, the time to show her what he felt. And she would be amazed. Elijah tied the canvas lunch bag to his belt and prepared to climb over the fence that separated the fields of Robin's family from his plot of land. As he went over the fence, he felt a tiny splinter enter his left thumb, but he just smiled.

The splinter was nothing compared to the wound he would soon suffer. His heart was beating heavily as he reached the combine. Robin was bent double, examining some part of the vehicle's underbelly. Her father and three farmhands looked on, not out of idleness, but out of concern. Elijah approached, blinking awkwardly in the sun and taking unnaturally small steps to avoid damaging the crops. It would not do to destroy the livelihood of his beloved's family while declaring his passion.

Robin's father, Ulysses Thickett, turned around to face Elijah. "Yes? What do you want?" Robin herself stood up, looking at Elijah with a puzzled expression. Elijah said nothing for a few seconds, which gave her time to notice the bag swinging from his belt. He suddenly came to his senses. "Mr. Thickett," he said, addressing her father but holding out the lunch bag to Robin. "Robin has no lunch. I . . ." There was a long, meaningful pause. ". . . was worried," he finished.

Robin did not respond. Ulysses Thickett did not respond. The farmhands stood and stared. Their faces all told the same story, but it took a few moments for Elijah to realize what that story was. The ending, he found, was not a happy one.

SUNDAY

From: Iphis
To: Thisbe
Subject: your story

Sorry—meant to reply last night. Tried to wait up for it, but didn't make it. But oh man! What a story! Poor Elijah. What a beating he took. You are the queen of foreshadowing. Have you been reading mystery novels?

But . . . I don't get the ending. What happened? Am I stupid? Did I miss something?

From: Thisbe
To: Iphis
Subject: Re: your story

Oh, it all just ends badly for Elijah. Yanno . . . I could work on it some more, but I was so worried about sharing it with my Audience (and the presentation—yes, I confess). But no, you not stupid. Me lazy, apparently.

From: Iphis
To: Thisbe
Subject: Re: Re: your story
Hmm. Don't know if I would call you lazy, exactly. Maybe you just needed some Audience feedback? Maybe authors have to share their work with other people, before they are sure it's ok? Anyway, you're off to a great start: your stories definitely have what Ms. Patinsky calls "substance." I don't know what the mystery substance is, but it's something good. It's nice and crunchy, I'd say. Want my honest opinion?

From: Thisbe
To: Iphis
Subject: . . .
gulps hard Ok. I can take it.

From: Iphis
To: Thisbe
Subject: no, no, don't panic!!!
You have Great Potential. I see no reason why you couldn't write a whole novel. I mean, you take that Elijah story and you stretch it, add bits on either side, add a few subplots and don't write "THE END" for a hundred or so pages, and you're set. I know you can do it. I can tell that you READ people. You WRITE people. You are already living in a novel with them. You watch them and you see

more in ten minutes than most people do in a lifetime. How else could you say so much about all those people who don't even exist? Or they didn't, before you wrote Robin, Elijah, Ulysses, and the three farmhands. . . . Writing well is seeing the world with stronger eyes and ears than most mortals have. That's what I think—speaking as your Audience and all. ☺ And I think *you* need that cape, mask, etc.—man, you have X-ray vision. You don't just see people; you see through them. I'd be afraid to meet you, if I hadn't already (sort of)! People must be terrified of you. Your teachers must be terrified of you. Do you know how good you are?

I loved your story.

From: Thisbe
To: Iphis
Subject: potential
Er *she says, taking off super-X-ray-vision goggles* nope. *takes off cape and mask to reveal a surprisingly small person with narrow shoulders and misbehavish, graggly brown hair that looks worse when she's brushed it* Thanks, Iph. *punches Iphis's shoulder affectionately* I appreciated that. And if you let me "doctor" (as my dad would say—PhD's are doctors, too, you know!) your email a bit, e.g., taking out the nice bits about me, I might quote it in my presentation—which is on WEDNESDAY.

From: Iphis
To: Thisbe
Subject: reality
Aw, shucks. . . . And sure you can use it (on WEDNESDAY?? Yikes!!! Ours isn't due until Friday). Doctor it however you like. I

took its pulse and peeked under its eyelids and can reassure you that my email will make a most willing patient. Grateful even (fix it up enough and we can put it in the final project, too. . . . I don't think it would count as cheating. We could say that this was a "Moment of great progress and authentic learning."). . . .

From: Thisbe
To: Iphis
Subject: Re:ality
grins to herself, looking forward to the delivery of a spectacular final project, with hardly any sarcasm in it Ha ha ha. May I change the subject (anything to put off thinking about school tomorrow . . .)? I've been thinking about that poem you wrote. And since we are friends now . . . how about we do an experiment? I want to see if telepathy is really possible. What do you say?

From: Iphis
To: Thisbe
Subject: . . . slightly weird
Man, you're weird. Go for it.

From: Thisbe
To: Iphis
Subject: . . . more than slightly weird
Thisbe puts one hand on each of her temples and closes her eyes. She frowns with concentration. She thinks hard. She wrinkles her nose. She wonders if Iphis secretly needs a hug

From: Iphis
To: Thisbe
Subject: Re: . . . more than slightly weird
Thinks: I'd love a hug. I was feeling pretty sad

From: Thisbe
To: Iphis
Subject: Re: Re: . . . more than slightly weird
WOW! Bizarro! I got you—loud and clear. You read my mind and I read yours. So sure, here's a hug. *hugs Iphis*

From: Iphis
To: Thisbe
Subject: . . .
hugs Thisbe back Thanks, buddy.

Week Three, April 16

MONDAY

I failed in my patrols of Cat and Dog Zone. Chutney got into my dad's office today. He must have known it was unclaimed territory. Chutney had a good nose around the piles of papers, books, and boxes that litter the floor/shelves/desk/all available wall space. I'd be worried about it but my dad won't notice, even though he loves Chutney about as much as I do. . . . His office already smells pretty stale. Funny thing is, when I caught Chut in the act, he looked totally at ease, as if he had every right to be in the office. As if he had some special, psychic connection with its usual occupant. He dropped his ears and looked at me with such big, innocent eyes that I almost found myself being sucked in. I fought back, however, evicting the animal, sniffing the air, and setting a few things straight before closing the door and marching him off for a talking-to from Gran. Guess her plan for the different zones didn't quite pan out. . . . Bless her. She's a whiz at noodles, but ruling the animal kingdom? Better luck next time.

Another email from Mom and Dad. They've been taking trains, which reminded Dad of a poem he once read. Now ALL of his messages are in rhyme. My mom is just being my Mom. Reading timetables, making phone calls, checking details (i.e., continuing campaign to be superhuman). My dad, as usual, lifts, carries, charms hotel clerks, and changes reservations without paying the penalties. This is how they travel.

TUESDAY

I was so happy to see Granny Ed when I got home this afternoon. Even with the evil mutt! We ran out for chocolate croissants. Then I hung out at home pretending to work on my Audience presentation, but mainly I talked to Granny about Iphis and the girls at school. They hardly speak to me these days. I don't like being at school at ALL. Maybe I should be homeschooled instead?

I also talked to Granny about my journal and how I would have to destroy it because I couldn't bear the shame if someone else read it. She said that I should think very carefully before destroying what I had written. Throwing my journals into the fireplace was *not* allowed, she said. Burning a book is a very bad thing to do (even if you have written it, apparently). I have thought about this and decided she's right.

RANDOM THOUGHT (based on recent Authentic experience at school): the more people I meet, the more I like my books.

Will I ever be popular? I thought I was. Or rather, people like me enough, I guess, but I've started wondering how much I like them. I do spend a lot more time alone than they do (excluding Fishy, who is glued to me these days—or me to him, if I'm honest). I just like my own company. Does that make me weird? Or does it make me an excellent author? Just imagine . . .

> **JOB AS AUTHOR**
> ONLY INTROVERTS NEED APPLY.
> Don't come for an interview—just go for a really, really long walk and think about it on your own.

Granny Ed had another of her "brilliant" ideas. She said that "in the interests of self-knowledge" (which I think means, "let's figure out why you're so strange"), we should do a personality test. She meant a test to see what kind of personality I have, not a test to find out if I have one. Anyhow, she swore that she knew exactly which test I should do. It had some acronym she couldn't remember ("but no, really, I know just what I'm doing, hold on . . ."), so we spent ages figuring out what words we'd use to search for it on the Web. I was treated to a little speech about perseverance (because I was REALLY annoyed and frustrated. I'm used to doing these things FAST) and how truly, truly amazing "the Internet" is. I keep forgetting that she didn't grow up with it. For me, it's like making toast. Do it tons of times a day because each piece seems so tiny, and before you know it, you've overdone it and feel slightly sick.

It turns out that this personality test is like doing litmus tests on people to figure out if they are acidic or whatnot. I could do one on Melinda, but then, I already know the answer. Meow.

So I answered a GAZILLION questions, and it basically told me that I'm an introvert (which does not mean I am shy) who feels a lot and is very perceptive. It also said that my personality type represented "less than 1% of the population" and that I would have "extreme trouble mating." Not a problem, I told my grandmother. I did not plan on doing any mating anytime soon.

WEDNESDAY

Today I write my journal entirely in the present tense, just to see how it reads. Maybe the present is ok, after all? I know I'll be thinking about things that happened in the past, but maybe it'll be more interesting to read afterward? Let's see. . . . Wednesday afternoon and here I am in English class. The mood is quiet. I'm leaning forward on one elbow, my head resting on my hand. My hair has dropped down over my eyes, and I am hoping desperately that the Bearded Wiz won't notice that they are closed. I'm afraid that if I open my eyes, I will be sucked into staring at the TV-interference pattern on his sweater. He must go to the same store as my dad.

About half of us are actually prepared for our *present*ations (ha). The rest have just shown up to class. Guess which half Melinda and Kel are in? They're up first. Melinda's fidgeting and laughing, barely looking up from her brief, hastily scribbled notes to give a halfhearted account of her half-baked project and its execution. I wince. I'd like to have *executed* that project a couple of weeks ago. I take a deep breath and picture myself in a bubble, floating just below the stained ceiling tiles, ready to use my robotic arm to fix an annoying, flickering fluorescent light. It's giving me a headache by my right eye. I sink a little lower in my chair and try to picture Iphis (tall, thin, blond?) steering the bubble with an enormous silver wheel. I wonder what kind of control panel the space bubble would have and where we might install the snack bar.

Kel finishes her half of the presentation (this would be the smaller half). I stretch my foot out into the space next to me. Nobody sits in that chair, now that I'm tackling this Audience project alone. My little boat has sailed away from the movie-watching odyssey that is Melinda and Kel.

Now David has stood up to deliver his speech. He's the boy who's always wearing his headphones to school. He's still wearing them around his neck, even in class, but Mr. Oliver is the only teacher who doesn't mind. His assignment is about reading aloud. The Audience he's describing is his grandfather, who is completely blind, but the rest of the class doesn't know this. I only know because David and I were put together for a project in math yesterday. I didn't care all that much about the math project (how could I?), but I was really surprised to find that I *did* care for David. He's quiet and doesn't like to attract attention. He wears cool vintage shirts, instead of those brand-new-but-weathered-looking garments from expensive stores downtown (I know I sound like my dad, but here goes: just imagine paying more to have clothes that look as though they've been dragged through a hedge backward!!). I see him walking along the school hallways, close to the walls, his eyes on the floor, absorbed by the music that's seeping out of those huge headphones clamped to his ears.

SIDEBAR: David didn't want everyone to know about his grandfather's blindness and his diabetes, but when I told him that I was doing my Audience assignment online, his eyes lit up and suddenly he wanted to talk, too. Perhaps he figured that if I was doing something different, I could be trusted. I made a joke about how math was evil, wicked, possessed: math was witchcraft in disguise. We should throw it in a river and see if it floated. He laughed his head off. Melinda and Kel wouldn't have laughed, but he did. And there he was, totally relaxed with me, talking about his grandfather, his life story, and his blindness. It made me think of my dad, writing about John Milton's blindness. I listened really carefully because the story seemed so important to David. He even put his headphones down for a minute. I wondered if this was my first step in a long career of being considered unusually trustworthy by strangers.

BACK TO THE PLOT: Now David speaks to the class about reading aloud. He speaks from his notes, very slowly. He's talking about his perceptions of an audience for a book the Audience cannot see. How the story is spoken aloud so he makes his voice a performance of it. David stands on one foot, shifts to the other, then back again. He doesn't look at the other students, not even me: only at Mr. Oliver, and then only occasionally. He gives nothing away. Mr. Oliver smiles at David from his chair, which is set to one side of his desk today. I guess he sees himself as our Audience on this one.

Melinda and Kel whisper to each other as David speaks. Melinda is drawing. Mr. Oliver hasn't noticed, which is just as well because Melinda is drawing him. She is a skilled artist with the amazing knack of bringing out a person's worst features. I lean to the left and rest my head on one elbow, so I can see her drawing. There's gangly Mr. Oliver perched on his chair, his arms and legs at odd angles, his knees and ankles all pokey. His new beard is vast and dense, threatening to engulf the lower part of his nose. His sandy hair falls forward. He looks more like a tall, scruffy dog than a Wizard of Literature Land. Of course, she couldn't resist drawing his patterned sweater. In her drawing it looks even more hideous than in real life (which I am forced to admit is quite an achievement).

Oh no. Now she's drawing David. He's appearing stroke by stroke while Melinda and Kel laugh under their breath. They're confident that I'll say nothing.

There's David's too-long hair like a troll, his glasses on the end of his nose, precious headphones around his neck. I'm furious. I don't want to cause trouble but this is so unfair. I can't speak up because if I do, David will know what they're doing. If I say nothing, there's always a chance that he'll never find out, get a B+, and go home happy at the end of the day. He'll imagine that for once, nobody bothered him. Today, he was allowed to go about his world in peace.

My mind wanders. My cheeks are flushed. I think about what Granny Ed would do and keep my mouth shut. I can tell David afterward that I liked his presentation. Mr. Oliver clearly does, and he is the person who really matters in this classroom. Why do people always want these girls to like them? They used to like me and I sure don't feel lucky.

Now it's my turn. I'd better come up with something to say, and fast. I stand up and get ready to speak from my notes. I look at Mr. Oliver. I take a deep breath. I begin, listening to the words that come out of my mouth. As the other students look up at me, I think "Is that really me who's speaking?"

THURSDAY

Bustory #1

It takes me twenty minutes to reach the pool by bus. My nose is stuck in a novel from the minute I pull the transfer out of the machine. This is a special book, not just something I took out of the library on a whim. It is my own, a trusted friend with wilted pages and a spine with a deep crease in it. I have a bad habit of rolling the pages over as I read. My favorite books look like telescopes and have a resale value of nada.

"Bad, bad, bad!" Granny Ed tells me off every time I pull another mangled novel out of my bag.

"I can't help it," I tell her. "Tough love, Gran."

"Right, but this book has grown up already," she answers,

quick on the uptake as ever. "It doesn't need tough love from you, pet." She smiles.

I think of this conversation again as I read on the bus. I look up for a second, without loosening my grip on the novel. Nobody else's grandmother is watching me abuse it, so I carry on reading. My mind is dancing as I read. My body is quiet, but my mind is turning somersaults and pirouettes, flying; sparks and flashes of color appear before my eyes, even though they are open. Left to right and up to down, they scan the pages. Words resonate. I *own* them. I taste them, speaking silently in my mind, loving them, relishing them, and visualizing them on the page. They are my allies, my subjects. My kingdom.

The bus turns into the loop. I've arrived. I swim for a reason. I haven't swum in a few weeks, which is a long time for me. There's a reason for this, too.

Once inside the changing room, I get ready quickly, as quickly as I do everything else. Abracadabra, and I am done. Into the shower and through to the indoor-pool world of shiny tiles and sleek swimmers. The tiles are smooth under my feet. Takes me a second to realize why. I have forgotten my pool shoes. That's what happens when my mother goes away. She is my external hard drive. My extra can of memory. "Don't forget your pool shoes." Guess what? I forgot my pool shoes.

It's been so long since my last swim that I've lost the habit. I start with my usual ritual. Tip head over, slink into cap, tuck curls in, fix goggles, pull strap over the top, tweak cap over ears. Stretch, swing arms, head to pool. Hesitate. What? Hesitate? I never hesitate. What am I doing? I jump right in. I'm the immediate jumper-inner. No waiting, no testing the water. Something has changed, but nobody else can tell.

For me, swimming happens between my ears. It is a spiritual experience. It's one of those rare times when my brain slows down, no longer racing in circles, seeking words, phrases, ideas, images, and sounds. My mind steadies itself. My brain says ticktock, ticktock, breathe in, breathe out, calm, calm, ticktock. As my head rises, I hear the shouting, the splash of boys dive-bombing into the pool from the five-meter board, the yell of "JUMP! DO IT!" and the occasional firm voices of the lifeguards. Underwater, I hear nothing but the sound of my own breath. My goggles are misty, and I feel as though I'm swimming in clouds. I wonder why we don't call them foggles? But under the water, my vision is clear and so is my mind.

I am overtaken by a man swimming a messy crawl. I don't think much of messy swimmers. I concentrate and take pride in my stroke, focusing on the timing and the way my arms reach out ahead of me. When I slow down, I let my feet dangle downward. I picture myself as a sleeping dolphin. I believe that humans need water for grace and ease. I believe that this messy crawler is spoiling my concentration, and I swim around the bubbles and choppy water he has left in his wake.

RANDOM THOUGHT: Why don't people make waterproof

notepads for swimming novelists? I can't possibly write down later all the ideas that come to me when I'm swimming.

I can't keep this present tense thing up. I'm going back to the past. Or rather, "I went back to the past tense." Ha ha ha.

Anyway, that was my first swimming trip in a while. At first I couldn't. Then I wouldn't.

It was strange to be back in my swimsuit. My body felt different, but maybe it was all in my mind? Granny Ed would have given me another long stare. "Body and mind are two sides of the same coin." [Cue: soft yoga-teacher-type voice and floaty music.] "You cannot think with one without using the knowledge of the other." Yeah, yeah, that's helpful.

Somehow, my body wasn't thinking right. It felt wrong, and it told my mind ALL about it. I stared at my stomach to see if it looked different. It didn't seem to, and nobody pointed at me. Nobody noticed that I was the weird girl who'd gone swimming in a mind and a body that didn't match.

Today I was swimming automatically. My body was doing the same things it always does, but my mind was racing ahead of my limbs as I stared at the lights glowing greenly at the bottom of the pool. It was only when I got to the end of the lane and grasped the side, panting, that I realized the lights were actually orange. I was swimming with my body but not my head. I couldn't stop myself, couldn't regain control of the chattering in my mind.

I did my minimum number of laps and pulled myself out with my arms. That was when suddenly I realized how great it was to be free, to have my body back temporarily. To slip into my suit and not say horror, horror, horror.

That last part is from *Macbeth,* by the way. With both my parents being English profs, my dad says, "Horror! Horror! Horror!" every time he burns toast. So we hear that phrase a lot in our house. My dad's a disaster with appliances (see earlier comment about our Very Serious Rules For Dishwashers, etc.).

Normally I swim with my mom. We've swum together as long as I can remember. Since I could swim, probably. My dad, on the other hand, plays tennis with a friend. My parents also like to walk together. They hold hands. They used to hold my hand, when I was little—not now, though. Now they hike on their own, and I usually do things with my friends. My friends swim, too, but it's a different kind of swimming. They swim so that they can talk to each other. I swim so that I don't have to talk to anyone. So that I am disguised and nobody knows me. I did like spending time with my girls, but my ideas have changed. Or maybe theirs have. Or maybe we've all changed, in different ways?

BACK TO THE PLOT: Yesterday I did my progress report about my Audience. It went pretty well. I talked about sharing my writing with someone I'd never met and having my own personal critic. I told the class that it wasn't like giving my work to a teacher because it wasn't being graded and because the Audience doesn't always wait until my stories are finished. My Audience sees the half-finished scraps of ideas and listens when I talk about the process—how it's hard to get started, how it's even harder to finish, and how BADLY I want to write something more interesting than my parents do. It's not that I think their writing is boring. It's just that I want to be the person who writes the stories. Not a person who tells her audience what to think about other people's stories. Right now, my parents are in Canterbury, hot on the trail of Geoffrey Chaucer. What a thrill.

Another group is reading manga translated from Japanese into English. They asked, "Are we the Audience the authors had in mind?" Four girls are working on some Young Adult series together. Two boys are doing something about *Dune*. Mr. Oliver seemed really pleased with our work, but he was being generous to some of the groups, I think. We talked about the age of a book's audience, their gender, location, and language. He asked us what effect all of these things have on the contents of a book. He asked us, "What's an adult book and why?" That kept us quiet for a few minutes. I don't think anyone had given that much thought. He asked us, "What's Young Adult fiction?" Then he added, "and I don't want to hear about gang fights, crushes, crashes, and underage sex!" Some people laughed at that. Those were the only answers they had in mind. Class was coming to an end by that point. I saw him glance at the clock as he launched into his favorite trick: ask a ton of really difficult questions right before the bell rings. "Why do you read a book? Is it the same reason you'd BUY it? How does a book get in your hands? What happens to a book after it's written and before you can buy it?" I thought they were great questions. I'm going to think about them.

From: Thisbe
To: Iphis
Subject: Grrr . . .
I'm angry today. Went for swim to calm down. Here's why . . .
When my mom is here, she helps me put goopy stuff on my hair to calm it down (my hair is only just past my shoulders, but it has a mind of its own). My mom isn't here at the moment, so I didn't bother gooping it. Too lazy. Today at school, Melinda started laughing about how my hair looked like a bird's nest. I was really angry but I didn't know what to say. My mom would probably say that Melinda was jealous, but if she is, she's hiding it very well. . . . Big sniff . . .

From: Iphis
To: Thisbe
Subject: Re: Grrr . . .
Hey, don't feel bad. My friends don't understand me, either. They don't even know I write poetry. And they DEFINITELY don't know about my strange obsession with Greek mythology.

From: Thisbe
To: Iphis
Subject: Re: Re: Grrr . . .
pauses to untangle her hands, a pen, two sandwiches, and a few small birds from her hair Are you joking?

From: Iphis
To: Thisbe
Subject: hidden passions

Nope. I keep my passions secret. My friends are from the basketball team. They are cool. They don't need to know about it—they'd probably laugh. The funny thing is, I have a favorite orange fleece jacket and every time I put it on, I think to myself, "Ha! It's the Golden Fleece," like in the story about Jason and the Argonauts. They have no idea at all. That's why I took this assignment. I thought I might be able to tell someone about my fascination with the Gods of Olympus!

From: Thisbe
To: Iphis
Subject: Re: hidden passions

Your secret is safe with me, comrade! But wow—it sounds as though you fell into that story and couldn't get out, ha ha ha.

From: Iphis
To: Thisbe
Subject: hidden passion fruit

That's me in a nutshell (which I can't get out of, either—which makes me a NUT). But anyway, I meant to ask you: What kind of dog is Chutney?

From: Thisbe
To: Iphis
Subject: Re: hidden passion fruit

The happy, bouncy kind

From: Iphis
To: Thisbe
Subject: or maybe a kiwi?
No, dummy! I mean what BREED!!! *looks perplexed . . . surely she isn't that clueless*

From: Thisbe
To: Iphis
Subject: or even a banana
You are right! I am waaaay MORE clueless than that. Chutney has no breeding. Or really, I can't spell the name of his breed. I'll look it up when I get a chance. One with not enough vowels in it, and everyone always pronounces it wrong (so says Granny Ed).

From: Iphis
To: Thisbe
Subject: you are the banana
You need a pet attitude makeover, girl.

From: Thisbe
To: Iphis
Subject: presentation
WAIT! No more of this dogchat. Meant to tell you that I gave my report thingy yesterday. It went pretty well. Everyone else is reading a book—mostly in groups—or watching the movie adaptation of an Important Work. There are some others working on the blog option, too. First they had tried the impossible option (c), i.e., pathetic excuses and wimping out, but Mr. Oliver wasn't having it.

Here's what I said: I told everyone that I was sharing my writing with you and that you were giving me great feedback and lots of encouragement. I also talked about truth and fiction and where stories come from. I said it was really helpful to have you reading for me—that once I get started, it really is just like falling off a log. Oh, and I finished up with a bit about how we were organizing our final project: my writing, your comments, a summary of our Authentic Learning, etc. etc. Made it sound as though we'd done a lot more than we have—*the usual*.

I also told them that I get my characters' names from junk mail. They all laughed at that. They didn't laugh about my X-ray goggles, about us being in Thisbe's Kingdom, or about words being my subjects, however. Mainly because I did NOT mention any of that. And I didn't tell them that it means the world to me that you are doing this. I also kept my lifelong ambition a secret—made it sound much more low-key: "You know, I'd really like to write— like—professionally—y'know, maybe—one day . . ." I confess I may have translated some of my presentation into Teen Speak. . . . I'm such an impostor.

My Classroom Audience behaved very well. Nobody threw tomatoes. They didn't clap at the end, but they were quiet and Mr. Oliver smiled when I finished. That's always a good sign. I didn't smile back. That might give the wrong impression to my fellow students: that I had actually experienced some Authentic Learning (which I have—but they must NOT find out!).

From: Iphis
To: Thisbe
Subject: Re: presentation

Dear Impostor,

So Mr. Oliver will know that you have gained great insight and wisdom from Authentic Learning, but you will package it so that your classmates think it is just the same old, same old? Very cunning. Not to mention, difficult. But it sounds as though you did a great job! Thank you for making me sound so helpful and smart.

From: Thisbe
To: Iphis
Subject: Re: Re: presentation
You're welcome. It wasn't that hard, hee hee.

From: Iphis
To: Thisbe
Subject: *a great laugh booms from Mount Olympus*
And now I bid you farewell! I am logging off to toy with the fortunes of pathetic mortals. . . .

From: Thisbe
To: Iphis
Subject: *scuttles away and cowers under a small rock*
That sounds fabulous. Happy havoc-wreaking.☺

FRIDAY

Writing news: I tried forcing myself into my chair, so I would have to write another story. Didn't work, but I did come up with another comparison. . . . This time it has to do with sand castles, instead of labyrinths or origami animals.

Stories come to me in pieces, not from the foundations upward, in a sensible way. It makes me think of a child who's building a sand castle, with great big dollops of wet sand. She grabs sloppy, dripping handfuls of sand and adds them on the left, on the right, on the top and bottom with no method, no planning, just adding for the sake of adding, la la la. Little bits and pieces crumble and drop off when she is looking at the wrong side. My castle could be top-heavy or it could be about to melt in a big heap when the tide comes in—like my self-doubt—washing away all the work I have done.

Bustory #2

After my swim today I was sitting on the #10 bus, not reading, not doing anything. A woman wearing enormous bell-bottom pants and headphones got on. She didn't say hello to the bus driver. Instantly the policewoman in my head said, "AHA! She can't be from Vancouver. I bet she won't say thank you when she gets off, either."

The woman sat down in her huge flapping pants, right at the front. I looked across as music started to pound from her headphones. I frowned and looked out the window at the golf course. She was ruining my favorite, dreamy-bus-journey state of mind. A minute later, as we were rushing down Tenth Avenue, the woman turned her music up even louder. By then I was feeling invaded. Other passengers started looking up from newspapers and commenting to the strangers next to them about destroyed eardrums and antisocial behavior. At the next stop, the bus driver turned around in his springy seat:

"Can you turn it down?" he asked. The woman sensed that someone was trying to get her attention.

"What?!" she asked, way too loudly.

"WHAT?! EXACTLY!" The driver laughed and pulled away from the stop.

SATURDAY

My brain has been chomping on the same subject for days. I didn't want to, but I mentioned it to Granny Ed. It seemed like the "mature" thing to do. I hate how being "mature" means doing things that feel bad because SOMEONE ELSE'S conscience is jabbing you. That would be my mom's conscience, telling me I should talk to my grandmother, bond with her while they are away (I'm convinced that this was her intention, actually). My mom is emailing me every day, but I felt like I was ready to burst, so I exploded on Granny Ed instead.

I told her that my body felt weird and my head was swimmy. And that I thought this whole p8ri8d thing was annoying, and I felt like a baby wearing diapers. Granny Ed stopped peeling carrots and told me I should fight my fears by educating myself. I hate it when she says things like that—if she had said that a few weeks ago, I would have been really angry with her. But then a few weeks ago, I also wouldn't have confided in her. She took off her apron and put her shoes on. We walked to the nearest medical clinic. She brought Chutney with us. I burbled and complained all the way. She told me to "get a grip." I told her that people over the age of twenty shouldn't use expressions like that.

At the clinic she left me staring at some cable news channel on the TV while she scooped up magazines for "young adult women," which I guess I am. It's all stuff about sexual health, sex education, pregnancy, etc. and it's all in pink and happy colors. Did young adult women design those magazines? I don't think so. Every page would be BLACK if they had.

Having done my Gran E homework, I could now write "The Comprehensive, Great and Glorious History of the Tampon" (illustrated in color, in three volumes, unabridged). Too bad that's not the Authentic kind of assignment we get in science class. I also understand that I am supposed to experience a sense of "freedom" even while I am having my p8ri8d— although I haven't found anything particularly liberating about stomach cramps and having to wear a mattress in my pants (hey! That almost rhymes!).

The one good thing that came out of our little expedition (and the really, *really* awkward conversation with Gran afterward) was that I am in NO DANGER of needing to worry about contraception. No way, man! I definitely don't need that kind of help. Who'd want to have "intercourse" after the Diaper Experience? How on EARTH do women in movies look sexy? There is nothing sexy whatever about "becoming a woman." Ugh. Ugh and more Ugh. Extreme Trouble Mating. Just as well.

From: Iphis
To: Thisbe
Subject: a gift for Thisbe

Look, I drew YOU! Well . . . I drew a version of you. A version of you in my head. A version of you based on the tiny pieces of information I have about you. Like the fact that you love swimming. . . . How d'you like the makeover, Mermaid Girl?!

From: Thisbe
To: Iphis
Subject: Re: a gift for Thisbe

WOW!!! How did you guess that my hair looked like that? Er . . . it's a bit tidy for me, but I guess you caught me on a good hair-day. Looooove the swimsuit thingy, too. *drools*

Week Four, April 23

MONDAY

I'm back at school in the computer lab, ignoring the sunshine and trying to do some homework. It's lunchtime but I've come here to avoid making the most difficult decision of my life: whether or not to have lunch with Melinda and Kel. They don't know where I am, so they can't feel bad for not asking me to eat with them at their usual table. I let them get to the cafeteria before me, so I could scuttle away, behind the piano. Sneaky.

Earlier today, I was in math, working on a "problem." At school, where lots of things are given the wrong names—such as Authentic, for example—I've always thought this to be an excellent name. These questions are definitely a problem for me. I'm so bad at math, and to make matters worse, while I was furrowing my brow and chewing the ends of my hair, David was just plodding along. Problem Solving.

"Man, you are so lucky," I told him, spitting out the ends of my hair, and watching it sproing back up.

"What are you talking about?" he asked me. I guess he's not used to people calling him lucky.

"Math! I can't do this at ALL, and there you are, plodding along as if you knew the right answer from the start."

"It's not that easy," he said, scratching his eyebrows with his pencil. "I mean, I have to fiddle a bit here and there to find my way. It doesn't come with directions."

"I guess that's the point. It wouldn't be a problem if it *did*. But I'm not as smart as you!" I felt really defeated.

"Oh, sure, you're a real dummy," David told me. So encouraging! Then he asked, "What do you do? You write?"

"Uh-huh."

"Well, do you already know how a story is going to end when you start? It comes all wrapped up and neatly finished when it lands in your brain? One, two, three and it's done?"

He was clearly going somewhere with this. I could sort of tell what point he was making, but I thought I'd let him make it.

"Of course not!" I said, sounding more indignant than I felt. "When I start a story . . . it could go anywhere. It's more like I'm *following* it, not creating it. I find out where it's going, bit by bit."

"There you are!" said David. "That's just how math is for me. I discover the story as I go along." He paused. "I'm just a geek, anyhow."

"That's where YOU are wrong," I said, knowing I was lying. David looked at me as though he knew, too. I added, "At least you're the right KIND of geek. Math geeks grow up to be rich. Literature geeks get to starve in chilly apartments. I'd say you are on a way better path than I am, my friend."

I think David was flattered that I called him a friend, but he knew when to let a conversation go. So he smiled down at his notebook for a second, took a breath, and said, "Come on, Fiz. It's not that hard. Look here . . ."

TUESDAY

In the lab again, avoiding lunch with the girls. Outside, the weather is practically yelling that summer's on its way. The last of the soggy cherry blossoms have disintegrated. The tulips are drooping and turning brown. . . .

Suddenly ALL of our teachers are working on these Authentic Projects. How come everyone wants us to be Authentic now? What was wrong with the way we worked before? Wasn't it Authentic? Wasn't it *real*? The B- I got in math last year sure FELT real.

Now we have to do a group project in PE, too. It's called "Bodies in Motion," and our teacher says we have to write a report or give a presentation that is "personally meaningful." I know what mine would be. A personally meaningful, Authentic mime of a person with wild hair, crashing on a couch, watching witch-vampire shows.

STOP EVERYTHING: A poem—or half a poem—came to me today, in a flash of inspiration! You would never think that Mr. Oliver's clothes could inspire anyone (except to run away, screaming), but here it is. His TV-interference sweater made my day!

> Once upon a time
> In the Pacific Northwest,
> There lived a cowboy
> Behind a teacher's desk.

His pen was good
And his aim was true;
He could squish a run-on sentence
With the heel of his shoe.

He didn't gamble
And he barely drank.
He was good with the ladies
(although his fashion sense STANK).

His beard was thick
And his virtues were many.
He had a talent for grading;
That is, he never did ANY.

His files were a mess
And his pens were inky,
But he had an IQ of 400
Just in his pinky. . . .

That's all I have. Maybe, if I am lucky, inspiration will strike twice and the cowboy will enjoy some grand adventures in Extreme Stamp Collecting with Anna-Lisa.

It struck me today—BLAM!—that David really is a friend. I didn't see that coming. We were chatting about our various Authentic projects and I realized that I knew quite a bit about him. A lot, actually. He knows about me, too. About Iphis, about Granny Ed, about my parents being away, even my writing. It's funny, but I think this is the way it's supposed to be. You just spend time with a person and get on with whatever you are doing and before you know it, they are tied to all these tiny pieces of your life with invisible bits of string. But it isn't at all like being friends with Melinda and Kel. It's much more like being friends with Iphis, apart from the fact that we've never met. . . . Somehow it feels NORMAL. I don't worry what David thinks of me, and I can tell that he doesn't worry. Or he just doesn't care. Today David told me that his grandpa has nightmares and can't sleep sometimes. David takes care of him when that happens, calming him down on the phone. It was pretty brave of him to tell me. I didn't know that old people have nightmares. I thought those were just for children. And maybe Young Adults.

WEDNESDAY

From: Thisbe
To: Iphis
Subject: group thingy
Hey you! Are your teachers all into this "Authentic" group thing, too? What a hassle. I don't play well with others. This is not good.

From: Iphis
To: Thisbe
Subject: Re: group thingy
Yep! VERY weird. Now we have to come up with team projects in science as well. We have to think of a research question on a subject we want to study.

From: Thisbe
To: Iphis
Subject: Re: Re: group thingy
Oh, I see . . . like this random, shapeless, shifty, wiffly-waffly un-project that we're working on. Wait. I forgot: "Authentic."

From: Iphis
To: Thisbe
Subject: on the other hand . . .
Ha ha ha ha. None of the people in my group have the same interests, so we are all running really fast in different directions. FUN, eh? Right now I'm sizing up my teammates to figure out who the lone wolf will be that gets to do everything while I sit back and slack off.

From: Thisbe
To: Iphis
Subject: no, no no!
NO! Very bad Iphis! That person would be ME, so you don't get to do that. Promise me you'll do your part, ja? In our math group, it's just David and me. Thisbe-no-friends has found another comrade! Isn't that great? I hate big groups. A group of two is just perfffffect.

From: Iphis
To: Thisbe
Subject: crush?
David? Be David a boy? Do David have crushola on Fizzy?

From: Thisbe
To: Iphis
Subject: Re: crush?
YES, David be boy, but NO, David not have crusheroonie on Fizzy. Fizzy not available in that sense. Fizzy closed, not functioning, out of order, kaput.

From: Iphis
To: Thisbe
Subject: crushed
Ach, too bad. I was hoping we might talk about flirting. *bat eyelids*

From: Thisbe
To: Iphis
Subject: Re: crushed
No way! Flirting is strictly forbidden! And now *cracks whip* to work we go!

From: Iphis
To: Thisbe
Subject: squish
Bah. OK. Laters, dude.☺

I have revised my position on teamwork. On learning that David is a whiz with PowerPoint, I've discovered that I LOVE it! He's going to sort out my Bodies in Motion project for PE, and I'm going to edit his English assignment. As my kindergarten teacher used to say, "Really great sharing, everyone!" In high school they call it "cheating." I prefer to call it "Authentic Learning."

Melinda got new jeans this weekend. I swear her pants are getting tinier and tinier. Soon she'll just be wearing two little patches of denim. David suggested we make a "Melinda's Jeans" slide show, where her jeans get smaller and smaller until she explodes. He sounded deadly serious when he said this. He actually started planning out the screens on my math book, and I had to fight to get it out of his hands. He's not a very good artist, but that picture of Melinda with her jeans shrinking down her butt was pretty hilarious.

I talked to Granny Ed about David's grandpa. She said that old people do have nightmares sometimes. It depends on what you see when you are awake. Some people see too much, she said. I don't know what David's grandpa has seen in his life, but I feel bad for him. I feel sad for David, too, visiting the old fellow in a home three times a week.

Anyway, Gran and I got to talking about friendships and what it's like making friends when you get older. She said that "adult friendships are a bit different, pet." You still go out shopping and eat or watch movies together, but you also help when your friend gets a new job and can't pick up the children on time, or you help your friend's daughter get into college, speak French, or get her CPR certificate; or you help with ballet, homework, or boyfriends. You still do all the fun stuff, too. It's just deeper. Maybe a bit more like being family.

So was she telling me that adult friendships are better? That my girlfriends are stupid and shallow? I was dying to ask her but was afraid of what she might say. I might have to admit that I already knew the answer.

In the end, I just went for it. I learned another interesting thing about Granny Ed today. She is not like most adults who think that questions are "rude." She told me that I should keep on asking questions and the only time I should stop is when I am dead. Wow. Wish I'd been able to tell my 2nd grade teacher that. She always told me I asked "too many questions." My grandmother's a revolutionary! I let rip after that, asking a TON more questions about why adults have nightmares, how they make friends, and how they avoid losing them. I learned that adult friendships ARE different, but that she doesn't think my friendships are stupid (she didn't comment on my actual FRIENDS, I noticed). At least she didn't call them a "phase." My dad is always making silly jokes about "phases," as if I were a moon. He can be so stupid . . . although right now, he is being stupid and having a lot of FUN without ME.

THURSDAY

Granny Ed told me I should write about Melinda. I feel as though I'm talking about nothing else these days. That can't be good. But here goes.

Aaah . . . Melinda. She used to be fun. She used to be funny. Very funny. And bold, too. She'd say things that everyone else was thinking but didn't dare say, and she'd do it with such a big smile that teachers never got angry with her. The rest of the class would flinch, and the teacher would just laugh. She didn't use to wear the world's smallest jeans to school. Now she scowls as if she is auditioning for some awful music video. As if she wants everyone to look at her. As if she imagines that everyone is looking at her body, all the time. She never knows where that camera might be lurking, so every side has to be her good one . . . although she is about as thin as a bookmark, so she doesn't really have "sides" anymore. But why does she need everyone to know that she is available? It's gross. Even animals are smart enough to have a mating season. And since I apparently have *no* mating season (and I'm not a boy)(and I'm not interested in hair-straightening products or who got voted off the island this week), I guess I am no longer any use to her.

I looked at the boys today to see if they were interested in mating season. Couldn't tell. Maybe boys who are hunting look different. Maybe they don't spend three hours in front of the mirror every morning to show they are available. They all look so cool. As if they aren't even trying. And you know, looking as though you are effortlessly cool takes a lot of effort.

Lucky for me, I'm invisible. Maybe I am the same color as the school walls. Or as David. Chameleon Girl. The boys don't see me, yeah! They probably can't see me underneath all my hair, anyhow.

FRIDAY

From: Thisbe
To: Iphis
Subject: EMERGENCY!!

My writing has come to a complete standstill! My brain cells won't work! I have rubbed 'em and rubbed 'em together, and I can't even get the teeniest spark. I just sit there and look at my screen, and I can't come up with anything new. NOT A THING. I need more material, right?

From: Iphis
To: Thisbe
Subject: Re: EMERGENCY!!

Hmm. It sounds serious. Sounds like you need my "New Guide on How to Bring Thisbe's Inspiration Back to Life," only $9.95 with this coupon. Call the number on your screen NOW! Don't delay! Not available in stores!

From: Thisbe
To: Iphis
Subject: *reaches for phone and dials number, pronto*

Hello? Is this the number for "Thisbe's Inspiration"?

From: Iphis
To: Thisbe
Subject: *responds in best telephone voice*

Yes-hi-how-are-ya?! It sounds to me like you need to take out the garbage. . . . If you can't get the words out, the garbage has to go first.

From: Thisbe
To: Iphis
Subject: *thinks: and this was worth $9.95??*
What are you talking about? *looks huffy* Of COURSE I am taking out the garbage. My parents are away and my granny isn't doing ALL my chores. How else would she get to yoga seven times a week?

From: Iphis
To: Thisbe
Subject: this isn't total garbage—just wait!
I don't mean literally, goof! I mean in your brain! You must be thinking about other stuff. Man, you have to FOCUS or we will never get this thing done. *looks sternly at Fiz*

From: Thisbe
To: Iphis
Subject: oops
OH SORRY. A Met-a-phor *she pronounces the word slowly and importantly as if it is the first time she has said it* How silly of me. Maybe you're right—there's definitely garbage in my brain and I think it's beginning to smell. That's not just because I'm studying math (ack, witchcraft!), either. . . .

From: Iphis
To: Thisbe
Subject: Re: oops
What's up, girlfriend?

From: Thisbe
To: Iphis
Subject: Re: Re: oops
Oh. Ouch. Eeeuw. You know. Ick. Ooh. Ugh.

From: Iphis
To: Thisbe
Subject: no way!
YOU'RE KIDDING?! *stares in confusion*

From: Thisbe
To: Iphis
Subject: . . . .
Yepperoo. My p8ri8d started and I am STILL annoyed about it.

From: Iphis
To: Thisbe
Subject: oh
Oooh. Sorry. Did it hurt?

From: Thisbe
To: Iphis
Subject: Re: oh
Nah. Only my pride. I feel fat. I feel like a balloon full of water. I don't really want to be a "woman," you know? Be "mature"?

From: Iphis
To: Thisbe
Subject: Re: Re: oh
pats Fiz on back reassuringly It will get easier, sure it will.

From: Thisbe
To: Iphis
Subject: let's talk about you instead
Thanks. *humphs* Did yours start?

From: Iphis
To: Thisbe
Subject: *blushes*
Er . . . I'm trying to sound like my big sister, Sienna. . . . Wasn't that helping? I was hoping I could say stuff the way she does. It usually does the trick for me. . . .

From: Thisbe
To: Iphis
Subject: Re: *blushes*
Geez, thanks. *smiles stupidly* I know it isn't going to go away, but man . . . I hate it.

From: Iphis
To: Thisbe
Subject: Re: Re: *blushes*
Is that all the garbage? I am SURE you can handle that stuff.

From: Thisbe
To: Iphis
Subject: recycling
Oh yeah, sure. My parents being away doesn't exactly count as garbage. I mean, I wouldn't throw them out. Wouldn't even recycle 'em. They are coming back.

From: Iphis
To: Thisbe
Subject: Re: recycling
Mighty generous of you, if I may say so. . . . *very big grin* I haven't recycled my parentals yet, either. Come to think of it, I haven't noticed if they have those curly arrow things on them. . . .

So how about another suggestion? If I could pull your mind away from ickinesses—sorry, I don't really like talking about this stuff. . . .

From: Thisbe
To: Iphis
Subject: Re: Re: recycling
Oh, sorry! I didn't even think of that. *cringes* Me and my big mouth. Of course, let's get back to work. . . .

From: Iphis
To: Thisbe
Subject: an idea
Maybe you're writing the wrong way. Do you write *everything* on your computer the first time?

From: Thisbe
To: Iphis
Subject: Re: an idea
Yes. Why? I do all my thinking at the computer. I do all my writing at the computer. And most of my eating, when my parents are here. I don't sleep on it, though (except for once, after a road trip with my folks last year). Which reminds me, I really should scrape

out the granola crumbs and make some oatmeal.

From: Iphis
To: Thisbe
Subject: Re: Re: an idea
Mmm. Tasty. Why don't you try writing by hand? Maybe that will get your brain working again? I write everything by hand the first time. I got the idea from an author in England who writes his first drafts in pencil. Whole novels. Imagine.

From: Thisbe
To: Iphis
Subject: wow, kids in space
How long would that take? I'm trying to imagine my dad writing books that way—it takes him several centuries to crank out a single chapter—but ok. I'll give it a try. I'm not my dad and I write FICTION, anyway.

Besides, my brain could probably do with moooving a bit mooooore sloooowly. *all of a sudden, Thisbe is floating weightlessly in space, rotating gently in her antigravity capsule*

Fiz taps on the outside of Iphis's sparkling helmet. Plink! Plink! So what do your parents do? I've told you that both of mine are profs, yes? Very dull. I'm just going to float in the antigrav capsule for a bit. . . . Care to join me?

From: Iphis
To: Thisbe
Subject: Re: wow, kids in space

Oh, sure, that sounds comfy. *leaps into the air and pokes a floating water bubble* My mom is a social worker. She loves it. Always talking about her job. Mostly she works with younger kids. My dad isn't working at the moment. His position was cut, so he's going back to college. I think he wants to do something with computers but I'm not really sure. Neither is he, come to think of it.

From: Thisbe
To: Iphis
Subject: Re: Re: wow, kids in space
teleports herself and Iphis into antigravity spaceship on planet Znooch That must be hard. Poor him! Is he finding it difficult?

From: Iphis
To: Thisbe
Subject: Welcome to Znooch, planet of endless attractions!
checks out a pale purply-blue planet, gradually coming into view through one of the spacecraft's gigantic portholes Dunno really. He doesn't talk about work the way my mom does. Especially now.

From: Thisbe
To: Iphis
Subject: Znooch welcomes you! Please take a guided tour!
What do you mean?

From: Iphis
To: Thisbe
Subject: I mean . . .
Well . . . *pauses to swallow hard* he's not exactly here at the moment.

From: Thisbe
To: Iphis
Subject: *teleports back to Earth with a thud*
Er . . . ok. Is he away? *pauses with meaning*

From: Iphis
To: Thisbe
Subject: Re: *teleports back to Earth with a thud*
He's not on vacation. He's not away for work. He's not sick or in the hospital. . . .

From: Thisbe
To: Iphis
Subject: Re: Re: *teleports back to Earth with a thud*
Thisbe looks on anxiously, convinced that she has said the wrong thing and is about to pull both feet out of her mouth

From: Iphis
To: Thisbe
Subject: gone
He left us. He's gone. To Oregon, in fact.

From: Thisbe
To: Iphis
Subject: oh my gosh
He JUST left? I don't know what to say. I'm SO SORRY. That's so tough. *Thisbe pats Iphis on the back. She's feeling at a loss for words. . . . Not a comfortable sensation*

From: Iphis
To: Thisbe
Subject: Re: oh my gosh

relaxes under the comforting pats of Thisbe's hands Yes, he just left. Three months ago. It was hard that first month. It's hard for my mom. *chokes* My sister thinks it's just fine, but then, she's been speaking to my dad with daggers for as long as I can remember.

From: Thisbe
To: Iphis
Subject: Re: Re: oh my gosh

Speaking with daggers? That'd hurt. She must be angry.

From: Iphis
To: Thisbe
Subject: evil

She is. It's from *Hamlet*, I think—some scene about disappearing dads . . . or evil dads . . . or something.

From: Thisbe
To: Iphis
Subject: Re: evil

Is/was he evil before he disappeared? Did you all want him to go? Did your parents decide together? How does this happen? Am I asking too many questions? (Come on Fiz, take a breath. . . .) Sorry. Kel's parents are divorced, but they separated years ago. She has been visiting her dad at his house forever. I don't know anyone else that it happened to recently.

From: Iphis
To: Thisbe
Subject: share
It's ok. I probably need to "share." My mom wanted me to go to counseling but I told her no. I would rather talk to you.

From: Thisbe
To: Iphis
Subject: talk to me
Of course you can talk to me. And you could write poems about it all, too, if you are angry. I expect you are . . . like that poem you wrote. I just put them together—your dad leaving. The guy leaving. Sorry, babe. You need a break. That sucks. Don't stop writing.

From: Iphis
To: Thisbe
Subject: Re: talk to me
Thanks. *looks down at hands, takes a deep breath*
To answer your questions: My mom wanted him to stay if he could be someone else. He was really hard to live with, but I still wanted a dad. Sometimes you can be really angry with a person, but you still want him there because you love him. You can't choose. You can't just fire someone you love.

But there was too much yelling. I don't know what my dad wanted. Nobody can ever tell—my sister says he wants everything and the cherry on top. Then again, my sister wanted to throw him out years ago. She settled for throwing plates instead (it wasn't really a plate, but you get the idea—actually, I think it was a bowl). It's easier for her. She's 21 and doesn't live at home. She can live without seeing

117

this stuff every day, but I see my mom's sadness all the time. The wondering, the questions, the hoping. I'm still trapped here, keeping the peace.

From: Thisbe
To: Iphis
Subject: Re: Re: talk to me
That's a lot to take in, friend. You are wise. You have learned some things from a place that is different from my own.

From: Iphis
To: Thisbe
Subject: a different place
That's for sure. . . .

From: Thisbe
To: Iphis
Subject: Re: a different place
But what do you mean, keeping the peace?

From: Iphis
To: Thisbe
Subject: peacekeeper
My parents can barely speak to each other without one of them yelling. So I pass messages. Peacekeeping. A fine Canadian tradition. I hate conflict. Especially when there isn't any peace to keep.

From: Thisbe
To: Iphis

Subject: Re: peacekeeper
Keeping the pieces.

From: Iphis
To: Thisbe
Subject: Re: Re: peacekeeper
laughs, looks down again, smiles sadly, and reaches out for hug

From: Thisbe
To: Iphis
Subject: hug
Offers arms open wide for a huge hug, a special hug. This is the biggest and most comforting hug that has been offered anywhere in North America since January

From: Iphis
To: Thisbe
Subject: Re: hug
Thanks. Nice hug. I really appreciated that. Sorry if I sniffled a bit on your shoulder. I'm finding this difficult . . . and I can't exactly confide in the people at school. Not Very Cool, you know.

From: Thisbe
To: Iphis
Subject: Re: Re: hug
looking at soggy patch on left shoulder It's ok. You will be fine. I know it. And don't worry. I have a washer-dryer and I know how to use it (unlike the dishwasher—I'll be happy to blow your dishwasher up anytime). Unless you left mascara on my shirt— wait. Lemme check.

From: Iphis
To: Thisbe
Subject: makeup
No makeup, don't worry.
Dishwasher? Huh?

From: Thisbe
To: Iphis
Subject: Re: makeup
Phew. Lucky. You nearly got yourself into Big Trouble, girl! *smiles, tugs Iphis's sleeve in a friendly fashion* I sorta figured you were an earthy, no-makeup type of gal. Sounds like you might need a new set of buddies, though. Like me: Thisbe-no-Friends.

From: Iphis
To: Thisbe
Subject: no-friends
smiles, feeling better You have friends. You have me, anyway . . . if that counts.

From: Thisbe
To: Iphis
Subject: yes-friends
smiles It counts. Could you stay for a bit with your sister maybe? Sorry, forgot her name—isn't she close by?

From: Iphis
To: Thisbe
Subject: it's Sienna
I couldn't really stay with Sienna, no. She lives in a house with

about seven other people, and my mom would never agree to it. A person cannot live on lentils alone. Besides that, Sienna's on field trips for her geology degree a lot, so she wouldn't even be there. I don't know if I could handle living with her boyfriend, "Chaz," and his cronies. I guess I could go and stay with my godmother, but she lives in the San Juan Islands and taking the ferry is a real drag. Can't face it.

So here I am, with school and basketball and you. Basketball is good to forget everything, good for the team thing and all that— but sometimes you can't forget. Sometimes you have to remember and talk about it before it runs you down. *looks shy* I'm so glad I have you.

From: Thisbe
To: Iphis
Subject: hanging out
You have me. Too bad we can't hang out. I could use the company. We could get our assignment done lickety-split! In the meantime, let me email you a waffle with some blueberries. Careful! It's sticky (like Chutney, both kinds). Consider this an IOU for future outings. . . .

stand aside, coming through!

From: Iphis
To: Thisbe
Subject: Re: hanging out
YUM! Thanks! It was QUITE sticky. Good berries, though. You're not a whipped cream gal, are you?

From: Thisbe
To: Iphis
Subject: Re: Re: hanging out
Nah, no cream. Too lazy to whip up the real stuff and I don't buy the exploding kind. It's the work of the devil, you know.

From: Iphis
To: Thisbe
Subject: speaking of work
To be sure. Now . . . do we get to work?

At school today I decided that I am a chameleon. Chameleons don't travel in packs, do they? So that's me. The animal with no pack, no herd, no gang. Yikes. I hope that doesn't mean I am more likely to be killed and eaten! I need ground cover. I need an ally. Or I need vegetarian enemies. . . .

I've started writing my journal by hand, following Iphis's advice. I'm using a pen I found under my dad's knitting magazine in the living room. Nice blue but the ink is a bit dry. I think it's one of my dad's pens. He's always emptying the pens from his pockets all over the house. Drives my mom CRAZY. She wants to know why he can't just leave loose change everywhere, like everyone else's husband. She says if he did that instead, at least she could gather it up and buy herself

122

something nice! I am sitting at the kitchen table. Granny Ed is tinkering with dinner, humming quietly, while Chutney chews on something green that tastes delicious to him but smells terrible to me. I have my chair turned around, but I can still hear his gnawing frenzy. I'm getting closer to my topic, walking around it in circles.

Here's how I'd like to start my Audience assignment: Without a sense of audience, an author is just a person writing alone, for her own pleasure. The audience makes the text what it is. The audience's responses bring meaning to the work. For my assignment, I hope to show this through my own shared writing experiments, in which the audience will give me feedback along the way.

I pause to watch the picture in my mind's eye. I feel like a magician who has promised to make the bunny disappear, but I have no idea how to do it. The lights are bright, and the theater is small and intimate. It's lit up but gentle. Dazzling but kind. This is my element, and Granny Ed is making veggie lasagna.

I picture my reader's attention being drawn away from the words on this page. I picture my audience slipping away slowly, out of the kitchen and into a paragraph in someone else's world. As my audience evaporates into thin air, the scene is one of contentment: the girl with the pen in her hand, gazing into space. The grandmother with a wooden spoon and a flat pan containing olive oil, three cloves of garlic, and some sizzling onions that are nearly cooked through and transparent. Outside, the spring rain drips off the roof onto the porch. Chutney's still at work on his treat, holding it down with one paw and none of the grace, artistry, or creativity of his human comrades. Nope. He doesn't do artistry, but he's got his treat and he's really, really happy.

From: Thisbe
To: Iphis
Subject: hi ho, hi ho
Yo, chickie! Can't write much. Am really downstairs with Granny Ed. This pen thing could work!

From: Iphis
To: Thisbe
Subject: Re: hi ho, hi ho
Keep going! I'm logging off now. We're heading out early tomorrow morning—spending a long weekend at my godmother's house, actually. Back late Monday. Talk to you on Tuesday, yes?

SATURDAY

This is going to sound pretty weird, given that she's my grandmother, but it's really nice to hang out with a girl who's NOT my mom and whose brain hasn't been possessed by the evil empire of Boy. Ok, ok, ok. I know she's in her seventies. She's had boyfriends; she's had a husband and a family. She's not supposed to be into "chasing lads" now, as she would say. But she has different ideas about this stuff. Sometimes I think she's still fourteen herself, but then she comes out with something nifty, something wise, and it makes me like her more. Makes me feel as though, at last, someone is tugging on that cord from the mother ship, pulling me back in. It also makes me wish I could roll up her smarts and stick 'em in my pocket when I'm at school being called Frisbee by Melinda the Dirtbag. Argh. I'm not sexy and I don't care. I have more important things to do than be "sexy."

I have books to write.

SUNDAY

Characters I have named but not yet created:

  Lady Gwendolyne La Bon-Bon
  Peregrine Allsop
  Jose Felicio Da Banana
  Mariolina Yurkle
  Hugo van de Gubler
  Thomas Lickblade
  Winifred Whim-See
  Frank O'Phoan
  Archibald Thump

Chutney's running around the house like a nutcase. Mainly because he _is_ a nutcase. I keep hearing a loud "CLONK!" as he drops his treat. I'm afraid he's trying to hide it somewhere he shouldn't.

Week Five, April 30

MONDAY

RANDOM THOUGHT: If I do have a book published one day, who will be the first person to buy it? Where is that person, right NOW?

April 30! The outdoor pool opened, and I actually made it on Day 1, third year running!

Night swimming. It's dark outside and rain is falling gently. Underneath the water, Thisbe doesn't notice the rain and everything is calm. Below the waterline, the light dances on the pool walls, and there is nothing but silence in her head. Above the water, the cool, light rain lands on her face. She squints and the lights over the pool form stars between her half-closed lashes. She breathes in, cranes her neck, and tries to see the stars.

Occasionally, a teenage boy bursts into her world, dive-bombing from the three-meter board, leaving a violent trail of bubbles behind him. Thisbe wonders how their shorts don't come off on impact, but she doesn't stop. She just keeps going, her movements slow, her legs keeping time, regular and thoughtful. Something in her world is turning. She knows that there is nothing amazing happening in the night sky above her, but she feels that a switch *has been flicked, a dial has been turned, the volume or brightness in her small world has been adjusted. More metaphors. None of these mechanical things are any good, though. She pushes off the back wall. She pictures the jar and blotting paper she used in 3rd grade to grow beans on a classroom windowsill. Yes, that's it. Something is definitely <u>germinating</u>.*

TUESDAY

Found another of Dad's lost pens. I have something to write my journal with, and my mom will suddenly find that all those loose pens are vanishing by themselves. It might even teach him to be a bit more tidy!

Tonight was good. Gran's Norm-ish leftovers were delicious. Today at school wasn't nearly as tasty. It was very floaty. I should have been learning about equilateral triangles, but I kept thinking about Lady Gwendolyne La Bon-Bon and the dragon. She lives in a tower with a vast pile of books. . . . I knew that there would be something unusual about her relationship with the dragon, but I couldn't figure it out. Those stupid triangles kept destroying my concentration. Gwendolyne kept reaching for another book and POKE!, there would be a triangle, right in her way, catching the corners of her fabulously embroidered bedspread and the tassels on her velvet nightgown.

When I came home today, I saw three girls in my grade outside one of the neighbor's houses. They were sitting cross-legged, at the side of the road, talking and looking really serious. That used to be us last year: Melinda, Kel, and me. I wonder what everyone thought of us then, sitting on the curb while the traffic whizzed by, and moms in cars said to their children, "Oh, that's so dangerous. I hope you won't do that!" I guess we won't do that again, now. . . . But we couldn't, really. Melinda's jeans would burst before she ever managed to sit down. She sure has gone to the dark side these days. They'll be wearing those *ss-crack jeans when it's thirty degrees outside. You wouldn't catch me dead in a pair of those. Or, dead is the only way you would catch me: I'd asphyxiate in them in about ten minutes.

From: Iphis
To: Thisbe
Subject: night message
How are you doing? I'm back.

From: Thisbe
To: Iphis
Subject: Re: night message
Not badly. Staying out of the rain. Dull, dull rain. . . . You?

From: Iphis
To: Thisbe
Subject: Re: Re: night message
Much better. The trip did me good: big meals, walks on beach, discovered new candy store. The boo hoo with you was also a big help. *scuffs toe shyly on floor*

From: Thisbe
To: Iphis
Subject: no scuffing necessary
You are welcome, sweetie. Ack, I sound like my mother.

From: Iphis
To: Thisbe
Subject: Re: no scuffing necessary
Sound like your mom all you want. . . .
Iphis looks up from reading Thisbe's note and passes another one back, across the library table Fiz, what is your position on malls—and on shopping in general? I am sure you have one. . . .

From: Thisbe
To: Iphis
Subject: passing notes
Thisbe folds up her response and sends it back. She is diligently polishing her latest piece for Iphis's reading pleasure. It's her medieval bit, so she is in character with her pointed hat on. She is trying to avoid the wrath of the gothic librarian in tight black jeans and pixie boots Weeell, I don't go to the mall all that much. My position on malls and shopping in general is (are?): it's fun once I get there, but afterward I wonder if I have been brainwashed into

buying things. I like to look at all the pretty stuff with my mom, but it's a bit like having a bag of marshmallows shoved into your hands and then eating them just because they're there. You?

From: Iphis
To: Thisbe
Subject: marshmallow attack
Scribbling happily. The librarian may look fearsome, but he is really quite harmless and knows where to find some extraordinary vintage comics in the library catacombs. Iphis is not rattled by his interested gaze Hmm. Don't know that I've had that marshmallow thing happen to me before, but I do live in hope. . . . And me? I'm indifferent also. My mom isn't crazy about taking me to the mall, and I'm not that interested in going myself. Would rather be outside.

From: Thisbe
To: Iphis
Subject: Re: marshmallow attack
eagerly reading Iphis's latest note, adjusts pointed hat with veil that keeps falling into her face My, but you're a brave lassie! Library catacombs indeed! I always wondered what they kept down there. A librarian with a head of snake hair, I was quite certain. And that's funny—I imagined the librarian was a woman. But now that I look more closely. . . .

From: Iphis
To: Thisbe
Subject: marshmallow, a snack
quickly returns another note Join me? No snakes, promise. I'm

climbing into the tunnel beneath this very table. Dress warmly. I suggest boots also. The emergency exits are here, here, here, and here. . . .

From: Thisbe
To: Iphis
Subject: marshmallow strikes back
tosses hat, veil aside Slow down a second! My boots are a bit tight. Can't get the left one. Hang on. . . . *threatens to topple over* I think I've got it. . . . Bingo. Here I come!

From: Iphis
To: Thisbe
Subject: this is getting silly
strikes a match and peers at Thisbe in the gloom . . . dodging the muddy water dripping from the ceiling So let me guess . . . you don't wear perfume, either? *the catacombs drip drop, drip drop . . .*

From: Thisbe
To: Iphis
Subject: yes, isn't it?
looks left and right to be sure about the snake thing Not really. It smells like jet fuel on me. "Eau de 747."

From: Iphis
To: Thisbe
Subject: jet fuel
Vroooom. Very seductive.

From: Thisbe
To: Iphis
Subject: Re: jet fuel
She lifts up one foot, fishing out a bootful of evil slime and mud. . . . She is enjoying the deep, slurping sound it makes Do you do "fragrances"?

From: Iphis
To: Thisbe
Subject: Re: Re: jet fuel
No—it's all advertising mumbo jumbo. I don't need anything more than my own natural, waterfall-fresh aroma.

From: Thisbe
To: Iphis
Subject: waterfall!
turns to catch falling droplets on periphery of Amazonian waterfall Hand me the conditioner, would you, babe?

From: Iphis
To: Thisbe
Subject: Re: waterfall!
Iphis looks puzzled . . . shakes a few more centuries of mud and slime from boots, tosses them into the Amazonian undergrowth, which has suddenly and inexplicably appeared

From: Thisbe
To: Iphis
Subject: uh-oh, spider. . . .
*Picks cobwebs out of Iphis's hair and casually flicks aside a huge

arachnid swinging from her braid—Poof! Off it goes*

From: Iphis
To: Thisbe
Subject: Re: uh-oh, spider. . . .
Wow, that was nasty! Thanks for the cleanup. How'd you like the tour?

From: Thisbe
To: Iphis
Subject: Dank You Very Much
Great! Didn't know that catacombs were like that. Very dank. We are now luxuriating in the Amazonian Spa of the Century, eh? Conditioner, please?

From: Iphis
To: Thisbe
Subject: whistles in the shower
Spa of the Century? We are? Oh! We are. Aaaahhhh . . . ! *falls backward into the warm water, narrowly missing the sharp, jutting rocks*

From: Thisbe
To: Iphis
Subject: Re: whistles in the shower
Watch yourself there, babe! Sorry to nag—but . . . the conditioner?

From: Iphis
To: Thisbe
Subject: conditioner—oh, sorry

Oops! *spits out bubbles, H2o, and small yellow crustacean; pokes at an enormous lily pad floating on a thick stalk* Sure thing, honeypie. Here you go. All organic and shmectomacro-biologically proven to enhance the di-hidroxy-pheno-proteio-amino-follicles of your lustrous mane.

From: Thisbe
To: Iphis
Subject: Re: conditioner—oh, sorry
shakes water from her shining dark curls, now with added bounce Wow, thanks! I didn't realize you were scientifically inclined. *Smiles mischievously as Amazonian sunshine twinkles off her perfectly straight, white teeth. Zing!* Fancy a coconut? *Whips out machete from mysteriously large pocket on side of animal-skin bikini; thwacks coconut into perfect halves. CRACK*

From: Iphis
To: Thisbe
Subject: tasty snacks, NOT marshmallows
Here, check out these barbecued bananas! *tugs aside a fern frond to show gleaming BBQ and row of tempting looking 'nanas, sizzling on grill* Let us feast on bananas, chocolate sauce (now where did I leave it . . . ?) and coconuts and all kinds of freshly spiced dainties under the shade of this nearby *WHOOSH! It appears* rubber tree.

From: Thisbe
To: Iphis
Subject: tasty snacks, oh go on, just one . . . ?
What luck! I just happen to have a jar of chocolate sauce about

my person. ("Spiced dainties"?? What?) Here you go! Grab a hammock! *PLONG! Two appear* We can wash afterward in the waterfall pool.

From: Iphis
To: Thisbe
Subject: just the 'nanas, thanks
'Nanas'll be ready in ten. Swim first, dahling? *with total nonchalance, Iphis executes a perfect header, leaving not a ripple behind*

From: Thisbe
To: Iphis
Subject: Re: just the 'nanas, thanks
nods with approval—tidy swimmer, like it Nice job, Iph. Hang on—here I come! *SPLASH*

WEDNESDAY

I'm working on that medieval story about Lady Gwendolyne. I have almost run out of stuff for it. Haven't sent it to Iphis. For the time being I have decided to share it with my journal, and if I am feeling brave later, I will email it to my mom. Here's what I have so far:

Gwendolyne's hanging out in her tower with her nose stuck in a book. She is rather frustrated because men keep trying to rescue her. The would-be rescuers are unhappy and frustrated because there is a fearsome dragon that breathes huge menthol-scented flames at them when they try to get close. If they had any heart, they would be sad for the dragon because she has a terrible sinus problem and suffers from awful headaches. All they can think of is the glory that awaits them when they rescue the damsel in distress.

However, what the people in the village don't know (and what causes them to spend fruitless hours at the local pub chattering), is that Gwendolyne is not a damsel in distress. She's a damsel in a LIBRARY. And the dragon (whose name is Pearl, by the way) was hired by Lady Gwendolyne to keep away the villagers and the puffed-up, preening men. This dragon is not a pet. She is a salaried employee who is saving up enough money to see a doctor (don't call them "vets" or she'll burn you to a crisp) for her sinuses.

The thing is, Gwen is an avid reader, and there is nothing she loves more than to be left alone in her tower (which she built in "science and tech" class) so that she can devour books in uninterrupted bliss. Which works really well for Pearl, who loves nothing better than devouring people who don't respect the privacy of readers. If there's one thing Pearl can't stand, it's losing her place in a book. And for those of you at home who are wondering, the tower was NOT on the curriculum, but Gwennie used her incomparable charm to convince her teacher that it was a golden opportunity for some Authentic Learning.

Pearl is busy with her dragonly duties because Gwen's folks are out of town at a conference whose name is something like "How do we make money from books when the printing press won't be invented for another 300 years?" But Gwen isn't short of books to read, having convinced the local monks to copy out her favorite works for her. Some of them threw in the illustrations for free, which was nice; although a couple of them were a little saucy (the illustrations, that is, not the monks).

THURSDAY

Sent my Gwendolyne story to Mom. My stomach is in my shoes. What will she say? Will write more when stomach returns to normal altitude.

Later:

Went outside after breakfast to look at the sky. It has stopped raining, but it's still really wet and breezy. The sky has a memory and that memory is a dark, grayish blue, the color of slate. There was a spider's web stretching across our front gate. Raindrops were clinging to the threads like pirates to a ship's rigging.

FRIDAY

It's funny, writing my journal by hand seems more personal. I'm almost blushing. I feel exposed by my handwritten thoughts. They are naked, undressed, without a font to hide behind. And there's my hand again, moving across the page, my fingertips grasping the pen, firmly, with determination.

Anyhow, I got an email from Mom. She thought my story was good, so far! I am going to hold back and not get too excited until I hear her say this in person. People don't always say what they mean in emails, and she is my mom, after all. She might just be saying this because she's supposed to. But ok, I'm OVERJOYED! And relieved!

But underfed. Must find carbs NOW!!

SATURDAY

Melinda's mom, Janet, drove us both to a modern-dance class at the community center today. I was surprised that Melinda wanted to go: it's been a while. We always used to do this together. I want to say "as kids," but I still feel like one, and she seems like . . . not an adult . . . but something else.

We barely talked to each other in the car. There I was, with my chin on my hand, watching the neighborhood go by . . . watching her mom drive . . . watching a guy in the car next to us trying to untangle the wires connected to his cell phone charger. . . . The lesson was good. It was fun. Melinda was a bit more relaxed and silly, like her old self. On the way home, she wanted to know more about my English assignment and why I spent my lunch breaks in the lab, etc. She didn't exactly use the word "geek," but she was thinking it. She didn't seem impressed that Iphis and I were actually enjoying the Audience project. She said it sounded weird. She thought I should spend more time with people who were "real"; although, typical Melinda, she didn't actually say what SHE thought. She said that "other people" might think it was weird. So I couldn't make her explain her point because it wasn't really her point, was it? I was going to tell her that she should have an original thought of her own sometime, but her mom was giving me a ride home and it seemed a bit rude. Wow. To think I said that exact thing to someone else at school once. . . . Melinda sure thought it was funny when it wasn't directed at her.

I think Iphis IS real. Our friendship FEELS real. I look forward to talking to her. Her words are on my screen. I print them out and read them over. From her brain to my printer. What is more real than ink on the page? She knows what's happening in my life, and I am learning more about hers. I don't see Melinda's point at all.

Besides, does she think her relationships are real? What does she think her "Dude" wants from her? Nobody can tell me that they are the best of friends. I bet he doesn't know the first thing about her. I see her face when they're together, and it doesn't look like the real Melinda to me. That is, it might be the real Melinda under all that makeup and fluttering eyelashes, but I don't usually have a shovel handy (meow). All she cares about is that she can walk around with his arms draped all over her. They make me think of chimpanzees in the wild. It makes me sad, too. She is such a great dancer, so light on her feet and so quick in her mind. With those big arms flopping all over her, she can barely breathe, let alone MOVE. She barely goes to dance classes anymore. But then, she's almost stopped eating, too, so I don't know why I should be surprised. Dancing and Food both used to be right up there on her list of "10 Things I Love."

We always used to talk about what we THOUGHT. It was always about ideas and dreams. Now it's as if her dreams have stopped, and it's all about how people look and what they think of us. I can't control what other people think of me, so isn't that a total waste of time? I want real friendships. So I guess I'll just have to be strong. Until this year, we had no bodies. We had minds and friendships. Now it's all about how our bodies look, boys' butts, and *ss-crack jeans.

RANDOM THOUGHT: Why do bodies spoil everything? Why do you need a license for a dog, but you get a body like THAT *snaps fingers*, no questions asked?

Dear Secret Reader,

As I read over the last few pages of my journal, I am as delighted as ever with my choice of names for Melinda and Kel. Of course, those aren't their REAL names. I've never even met anyone called Melinda. How dumb do you think I am?

SUNDAY

I'm standing in the kitchen, in my pajamas. I'm looking out the window, munching on a slice of peanut-buttered toast. Granny Ed has been up for ages. She's already walked Chutney and been to a yoga class. The sun has risen as lazily as I have this morning. It's up, but it really couldn't care less. I'm listening to a news report on the radio, which is burbling on the kitchen counter. My parents always listen to the news, and I haven't bothered to change the station.

The sky is smiling and staring, smarting and bright after all that rain. There must be clouds, but I can't see them in the gleaming world beyond this kitchen. It is as if an artist has taken one big blob of oil paint and smeared it across the entire sky with a knife. My dad loves this kind of light. It puts him in a great mood and makes him want to grab a waterproof jacket and a pair of huge hiking boots. He has the most ENORMOUS feet. He'll take off on a long walk (with anybody who'll go with him) through the dripping woods, enjoying the mud and declaring "Joy!" at the smell of drenched trees, leaf litter, puddles, fungus, and ferns. He says it smells "so alive" to him.

I have to get the thought of a long, soggy walk out of my head. Right now, there's nothing I'd rather do . . . but I have to shake the crumbs off my hands, clean up, and do some homework. Too bad. Up the stairs I'll go, two at a time, and with the kitchen radio becoming fainter by the second, I'll slide into my chair and hit the power button. As I wait for my computer to come alive, I'll hear cars driving by on wet roads and a crow hunched on the power lines outside the house, squawking.

I can do this. I can. My computer screen flashes, the fan sighs. Here we are now, ready to roll. Here come the words.

From: Iphis
To: Thisbe
Subject: are you there?
Hey, you!

From: Thisbe
To: Iphis
Subject: yes
Ja? *takes break from feverishly writing all day*

From: Iphis
To: Thisbe
Subject: Re: yes
I'm looking out my window. I can see the Big Dipper. It's right there—looks like it's hanging right outside my house.

From: Thisbe
To: Iphis
Subject: Excuse me, but . . .
Did you say DIAPER?

From: Iphis
To: Thisbe
Subject: Re: Excuse me, but . . .
DIPPER. Man, you have periods on the brain.

From: Thisbe
To: Iphis

Subject: *winces*
Oh. What's it doing?

From: Iphis
To: Thisbe
Subject: dipper (not the sauce)
Er . . . dipping?

From: Thisbe
To: Iphis
Subject: Re: dipper (not the sauce)
Very funny. Let me look—hang on. . . . WOW!!!! It's over my house, too! Amazing.

From: Iphis
To: Thisbe
Subject: Re: Re: dipper (not the sauce)
It's really bright, isn't it? And to think you're looking at the same stars. I'm waving at you. See?

From: Thisbe
To: Iphis
Subject: waving at you
I see you. I'm waving back. So is Fishy. He's putting his twelve toes on the windowsill just to scare me. I always think he's about to jump. Or fall . . .

From: Iphis
To: Thisbe
Subject: Re: waving at you

Fall? Cats don't FALL, do they? They'd have to be pushed . . . and with twelve toes . . . he could hardly lose his grip.

From: Thisbe
To: Iphis
Subject: strange cat
You'd be surprised. I love him, but hey . . . he lost his grip years ago. He's not very bright (or as bright as you might think). Right now, he's looking up at the sky, getting ready to howl.

From: Iphis
To: Thisbe
Subject: Re: strange cat
That's one confused kitty.

From: Thisbe
To: Iphis
Subject: Re: Re: strange cat
He sure is. That sky is beautiful, though. I might be fixing to do some howlin' myself. It's so quiet here. Might be just what the neighborhood needs. The wind . . . the rustle of the trees . . . the delicate sound of Fishy and me howling at the moo-hoo-hoon together. Ah, on such a night as this . . .

From: Iphis
To: Thisbe
Subject: drops a big hint
. . . a girl's thoughts might turn to l-u-v?

From: Thisbe
To: Iphis
Subject: ignores big hint
They could, if that girl weren't ME. Yeah well, like, whatever you know. XD. Hey—it's late. You love those stars for me, 'k? I'm off to lie awake for a few hours.

From: Iphis
To: Thisbe
Subject: bye, dude
Okeydokey. Will do—take care of yourself. . . .

Week Six, May 7

MONDAY

Tonight, Granny and I watched a movie about a boy who gets to know a famous author living in New York. The author lives alone, like a hermit, and the boy needs someone to talk to about his own writing. It's funny how in movies, it's so easy to see WHY someone is a writer. The movie explains it all so neatly. I was really sad or upset, and one, two, three! I became a writer and everything turned out ok.

But it was cool to see someone in a movie doing what I do in real life and mostly in secret. His friends don't know that he writes. I can definitely understand that. I will have to clear out my locker very carefully at the end of this year. I don't want my little scraps of writing to go on any unexpected journeys.

Some people would envy me, I guess, because I have writers for parents. But my parents aren't real writers: they don't write FICTION. They write about writing. Or they write about the people who do the real writing. My dad says that professors spend so much time talking amongst themselves, that in the end, he's writing about other people who write about writing.

I just read that last paragraph and it's really confusing. I'm going to leave it here because it's what my mom calls poetic justice. That's what you get for writing books with titles like THE EPIC POETRY OF JOHN MILTON: HIS BLINDNESS AND HIS EYESIGHT. Or in my mom's case, GEOFFREY CHAUCER, FEMINISM, AND THE MEDIEVAL BODYSUIT. I dunno. Maybe one day I will appreciate their writing. But for now . . . I just don't understand why my parents wouldn't want real jobs, like being novelists. . . .

I should have known better than to let Chut wander around the house with that stinky treat. I found the remains under my pile of dirty laundry this morning. (I have been assembling it very carefully on the floor, at the end of my bed.) Maybe I should stop poking fun at my dad for being messy. That'll teach me. Now I really need to wash those T-shirts.

TUESDAY
From: Thisbe
To: Iphis
Subject: another story

Are you there? I have another story for you. It's about a character called Captain Corduroy.

From: Iphis
To: Thisbe
Subject: yet another story
Hmm. You like alliteration, don't you?

From: Thisbe
To: Iphis
Subject: Re: yet another story
No. I despise and disdain alliteration like a dark, dank December day.

From: Iphis
To: Thisbe
Subject: Re: Re: yet another story
Very funny, woo ha ha ha ha. I'm holding my sides! Tell me more.

From: Thisbe
To: Iphis
Subject: Captain Corduroy
It's about an amazing superhero. While his manner is gentle, his mind is mighty. Youngsters cannot spend a minute in his company without being stunned by the awesome power of his mind.

From: Iphis
To: Thisbe
Subject: Re: Captain Corduroy
Wow. He does sound impressive. I'm gripped already. I suppose

you're going to tell me about the origins of his superpowers, his wickedly cool weapons, his dastardly foes, etc.

From: Thisbe
To: Iphis
Subject: The Great Adventures of Captain Corduroy
Why yes, dear reader, I am! How very observant you are. And now, let me begin . . .

Captain Corduroy, Literary Superhero

Captain Corduroy was a superhero unlike any other. His teeth didn't flash. He didn't wear stretchy suits and he certainly never wore capes—they were *so* last year. He believed in starching his shirts. He edited manuscripts in every spare moment, and he always ate dinner at the same time, every day.

But in spite of his mundane appearance, Captain Corduroy's powers were awesome. Not only did he listen to stuttering teenagers at the dinner table, he had the gift of inspiration. Students who did not know him thought him a comic figure. But for those he had taught, he was heroic: he unscrambled their brains, bringing unbelievable wisdom and clarity to their otherwise foolish lives. Their minds were forever changed. . . .

FLASHBACK!

Captain Corduroy—or Archibald Thump, as most people knew him—was orphaned at an early age. His parents vanished after a freak storm in which their golf cart was crushed by a stampede of man-eating squirrels. After the malicious vermin had carried away their prey, all that was left of Archie's parents was a single argyle golfing sock. The nasty critters even took their SHOES! As an adult, Archibald still wore the slowly unraveling sock beneath his undershirt, as a reminder.

At the moment he learned of his parents' deaths, Archie was struck with a profound sense of guilt because he had not paid closer attention to them. He buried himself in books to relieve his grief. He read and he read and he read, until his library grew famous throughout the land. This library filled much of his Aunt Violet's home—she had taken him in. A solid, kindly woman, she adored her young nephew and had a passion for growing competition-sized (although rather strangely shaped) turnips. While not a great reader herself, she was a devoted subscriber to *Turnip Weekly* and always encouraged Archie in his passion for literature.

FLASH-FORWARD!

At seventeen, Archibald made the solitary journey to a university town. He was a shy, sensitive boy with a gentle manner, six boxes of matching corduroy pants and jackets, a year's supply of frozen turnips, and a U-Haul full of books. He never left. One might say that like his aunt's turnips, he'd struck roots. And there he turnipped along, completing his degree while the seasons came and went; his facial hair grew and shrank with the fashions, but his superhero suit never altered. Nothing but corduroy . . .

Archibald did not long for a crackling lightsaber or freezing powers in his fingers or death rays in his eyeballs. Oh no. Early in life, Archibald had recognized the power of the library card. He wielded his weapon with adult grace and strength. He no longer stooped; he looked people in the eye, and he spoke with majestic command. He was ready to wield his library card in the face of ignorance, cruelty, and any judge who failed to award first place to his Auntie Violet's superior, if misshapen, turnips.

But not everyone was impressed by his powers. One librarian

joked to her colleagues that instead of throwing him out when the library closed, they should dust his jacket and stick a bar code on it. In spite of being a high priestess to learning, this librarian resented Archibald's devotion to the gods of knowledge. She regarded him with venom every time he called up an obscure text from the library catacombs, and sneered at his back when he shuffled away with his loans. . . .

....

....

Ok, that's all I have. There still needs to be a battle scene (I fear that some violence may be inflicted on root vegetables), a love interest, and some kind of traumatic incident at the dry cleaner's.

From: Iphis
To: Thisbe
Subject: Love it!!
It's GREAT! I hope you keep going.
But don't worry about not finishing it. Bah. Endings. A technicality.

From: Thisbe
To: Iphis
Subject: but a question
Thanks. ☺ I'll do my best to finish it. The only thing is . . . Captain Corduroy is VERY similar to someone my mom knows. Someone she knows REALLY well. Ok, it's sort-of-kind-of about my dad. . . .

blushes horribly at the confession

Is my story still a story if Captain Corduroy is based on a real person? I couldn't show this to my parents because they'd guess who it was about. Will I ever be an author if I tell stories that are based only on real people?

From: Iphis
To: Thisbe
Subject: oh, that's easy
You shouldn't worry about that stuff, Fiz—where do you think stories come from? What matters about your story is the point you make with it. You didn't write down everything your dad said and did. You're writing from your memory, from what you heard, saw, and imagined. Then you grabbed your "doctoring" bag . . . and added the extra stuff (like the turnips, I hope). So *voilà*! This person is yours. The fictional version of him, anyway. Besides, you should just write what you want.

From: Thisbe
To: Iphis
Subject: I feel humble
Wow. You are so smart. I feel like a street performer, dancing really badly in front of a prima ballerina. That last email has to go STRAIGHT into our assignment. "Truth or fiction—and why it doesn't matter, either way."

From: Iphis
To: Thisbe
Subject: Re: I feel humble
You are picturing me in tights! That's flattering. ☺ And sure, we can put (most of) that email in our assignment. Without the tights, though. . . .

From: Thisbe
To: Iphis
Subject: anxious question for you
Sounds good! But what do you think . . . of my writing . . . so far . . . ?

From: Iphis
To: Thisbe
Subject: Re: anxious question for you
My perspective . . . as your audience? It's weird. When I get your stuff and print it out—as I always do, by the way—I don't feel as though it was written by you, even though I know it was. It's still you, but not the you I know. You sound like another person I know really well, but not Fiz.

From: Thisbe
To: Iphis
Subject: Re: Re: anxious question for you
Wow, that's weird. Not Fiz. Who???

From: Iphis
To: Thisbe
Subject: WHO
Someone older . . . It's as if you have a different voice or sound like a person I really respect who is older—wiser. If we were living in a Greek myth, this would be where I have to pay you for your tales with a gift of my fastest ship. I don't have a ship, so I'll just settle for saying thanks.

From: Thisbe
To: Iphis
Subject: Re: WHO
Thanks . . . nice ship! BUT DO I sound TALL????

From: Iphis
To: Thisbe
Subject: Re: Re: WHO
Yes, tall. Definitely tall.

From: Thisbe
To: Iphis
Subject: oh yes, I am tall
Ok, you are free to go now. Thou mayst go eat thy tasty din-dins.
she swoops away, graciously waving to her subjects

WEDNESDAY

I survived another day at school, the scene of the crime known as The Slow, Tragic Death of My Social Life. That is all I'm saying. I have more important things to write about.

More story ideas are coming. This is a relief. Maybe we'll be able to get this assignment done after all. Maybe I can edit our correspondence to look like a serious, thought-provoking meeting of teenage minds. If I were a real writer, I would need more than twelve weeks of ideas. This is a frightening thought. The ideas would have to keep coming, forever.

RANDOM THOUGHT: How many ideas will I have in my lifetime as a writer? How big is my imagination?

I wonder how I would measure it, if I had to. Do you measure your imagination in numbers, by the number of ideas you've had, or do you measure it in space . . . like a huge, empty room that is gradually filled with people and things, a big props department in your brain? Or do you measure it in time: time passing, time spent writing? I wonder who I could ask about this. I don't want to tell Iphis. I am pretty sure we are good friends now, but even she might think this was weird. Maybe I will ask Gran.

I heard from Mom and Dad again. Granny Ed doesn't have an email account so they send messages to her through mine. My dad's messages still rhyme but not as much as before. I think he's (ha ha good train pun approaching) running out of steam. Oh. I'm as bad as he is.

I've told them about David, but I must admit, I hardly mentioned Iphis. Somehow, she got only one line. They seem glad that I have become friends with David. Mom knew that things were a bit weird at school before they left. Everything with Melinda and Kel was changing, and I didn't know why. So Mom is happy that David is also around to give me someone to talk to about other stuff, help get my work done. Dad stays out of this. These emails just come from Mom.

The weird thing is, I feel really close to Iphis! Kind of like a sister, but closer. I don't know how to describe it. I feel as though we are in our own tiny bubble, separate from the rest of the world, as if we could float through the crowds at school, pointing at all the people and their funny clothes: how they try to look cool, leaning on their lockers and flicking their long hair, fiddling with those little toys attached to their shiny cell phones. And nobody would see us. There we'd be, flying invisibly around the hallways with nobody to bother us. We'd fly past Melinda the Lovestruck Puppy and Her Human Popsicle (I must have some oxygen delivered), past those girls with the too-shiny black hair, out into the world and freedom, away from Fluorescently Lit Learning Land.

Don't be scandalized, dear reader: her name isn't REALLY Melinda, remember?

But is it normal to feel this way about Iphis? Is it weird to feel this close to another girl? This is confusing.

I know I feel something, but I don't know what that something is.

THURSDAY
From: Thisbe
To: Iphis
Subject: boy stuff
Hello? I need to talk. . . .
So Melinda describes her boyfriend to anyone who will listen—and that seems to be everyone—except me, of course. She really likes to show off. Today she described Lucas as "the paragon of masculinity." Her friends smile so knowingly, but I'm not sure how much they do know—not the meaning of "paragon," certainly, and I don't know how much masculinity they've seen, either. They all say they've had sex, but only Melinda talks about it constantly. If she is to be believed (which she isn't), she has tried everything, done everything, and knows where to get the T-shirt. It's naaasty.

From: Iphis
To: Thisbe
Subject: Re: boy stuff
What do you mean by "everything"?

From: Thisbe
To: Iphis
Subject: Re: Re: boy stuff
COME ON! You know. Do I have to spell out s-e-x for you?? Ok, well I have. Spelled it, that is, not had it. Me, I'm not interested—

yet. *million-dollar question approaches stealthily, like a thief in the night*

So, have you? What was it like?

From: Iphis
To: Thisbe
Subject: tangent!
Ironic bus moment!! I was getting on the bus this morning in a huge crowd—downtown, on Granville. A Native American couple was sort of ahead of me, but it was really difficult to see whose turn it was. We arrived at the bus doors together.

"Go on," I said. "You were here first." So they did.

A few seconds later, I realized what I had said. I think they did, too.

From: Thisbe
To: Iphis
Subject: Re: tangent!
Great bustory. But I can hear you stalling!!! COME ON, DISH! *looks menacing, but winks right away*

From: Iphis
To: Thisbe
Subject: back to boy stuff
Thisbe, you push me! I'm blushing! Why do you think you're absolutely the last virgin on the planet? It's amazing that I can't see your halo shining from here. *waves madly from the wilderness that begins at Main Street* Well, let's see. I haven't met the one and only person with whom I want to do that

special everything yet. . . .

But just to clarify—by "everything" do you mean the biological entanglement part? Or do you wonder if I have lain naked in a bath filled with ass's milk at twilight in Cairo . . . while my beloved brings spiced dainties in copper bowls for me to eat . . . ? In either case, no.

From: Thisbe
To: Iphis
Subject: even I don't use expressions like that
SPICED DAINTIES??? I've been meaning to ask you about that. You challenge my vernacular, girlfriend.

From: Iphis
To: Thisbe
Subject: Re: even I don't use expressions like that
I'm hurt! *feigns surprise, winks* You didn't even comment on my purple prose!

From: Thisbe
To: Iphis
Subject: . . . and I'm a word geek
Oh, sorry. :-/ It was very purple. Positively purple. Guaranteed to make readers squirm in their sneakers. Really, though—you haven't?

From: Iphis
To: Thisbe
Subject: word geek

Nope, but hey, it's not all that romantique. My father plans to sell me to my beloved's family (the exporter of spiced dainties, in more ways than one) for a couple of camels. . . .

From: Thisbe
To: Iphis
Subject: to contestant number one
Ha-ha-hardly. If you were sold at a market in exchange for livestock, which kind of livestock would you go for and why? And that goes to contestant number one.

From: Iphis
To: Thisbe
Subject: contestant number one responds
You watch too much television! Well, Shnookie, it would have to be a white pony, because I have lily white, silky smooth skin and I looooove to horse around.

From: Thisbe
To: Iphis
Subject: Re: contestant number one responds
Ffffunny. Know what? I think I might be asexual. Really. Mating rituals don't appeal to me. Remember the pitchfork and the hay bale? I don't see it. No sexual imagery. No sirree.

From: Iphis
To: Thisbe
Subject: Re: Re: contestant number one responds
Seriously? I pictured fights breaking out over you. Swords at dawn—the whole bit.

From: Thisbe
To: Iphis
Subject: *coughs modestly behind hand*
Well, I do look quite good. . . . I may not be cut, but I'm not entirely lazy, either . . . *flexes impressive biceps* and I do want people to look at me, I think. I just don't necessarily want to be touched. I'm like one of those dummies in shop windows.

From: Iphis
To: Thisbe
Subject: shop dummy
But you're no dummy! Ha ha ha . . . but seriously . . . wow, that's different. . . . I mean, I'd love to have sex one day. On more than one day in fact.

Don't boys look at you all the time?? Course they do *smiles am I right or am I right*

From: Thisbe
To: Iphis
Subject: Re: shop dummy
cracks her small but deadly grammar whip—kchaaaah Hey! Where did all your punctuation go? But of course . . . and between us girls . . . my friends say that none of the boys ask me to get frisky because I have this expression on my face. *doing it now* Can you see it? It says "come any closer and I will eat you!"

From: Iphis
To: Thisbe
Subject: you scary thing

Men on toast! That's hardcore. Maybe we need to send you to finishing school so that you can learn to smile—instead of BITE.

From: Thisbe
To: Iphis
Subject: Re: you scary thing
Finishing school—yah!—that'd finish me off. But learning to balance books on my head would be a nifty party trick. What's your favorite look then? Come clean! Are you grunge? Sexpot? Is your hair, like, purple or something? Do you wear those butt-crack jeans? *shivers at how uncomfortable they look*

From: Iphis
To: Thisbe
Subject: Re: Re: you scary thing
Purple like my prose, ha ha ha. But wait: did you say "LIKE purple or something?" Have you been, *like*, possessed or something? Gotta go. Mom is calling—needs help with dinner, she sounds tired—can you hang on??

From: Thisbe
To: Iphis
Subject: *waits*
Yep

From: Thisbe
To: Iphis
Subject: *waits some more*
time passes
time passes
time passes

◇ ◇ ◇

Time passes and Iphis doesn't return. She's sweet to notice when her mom is tired like that. I should be so nice to my mom. Maybe I am. She tells me that I am "one in a million," but I haven't figured out which million yet. Maybe all mothers say that?

This sex stuff is strange. I'd watch movies with my friends (back when I knew who my friends WERE), and we'd all get hot and bothered and silly. And then someone would say, "Hey let's go up on the roof and watch the stars," and we'd all go up there and lie on the gravel like old, old philosophers, not like teenage girls who've been laughing at some stupid movie and trying to figure out if we like the main character's butt. I mean, who knows what to like about a butt, anyway? A butt's a butt and you sit on it. Right? I've got to be missing something.

Anyhow, I sit and watch those movies alone now, and I wish that was me, sitting next to a guy who looks at me so tenderly and . . . I never get to the next part because I've never actually kissed anyone, so it's kinda foggy. Like looking through foggles. Don't really know how to imagine it. Can I EVER be a novelist if I can't imagine one lousy smooch?

RANDOM AND <u>VERY BIZARRE</u> THOUGHT: One day my characters may want to . . . you know . . . have sex with each other. Like . . . wow.

But I do want that stuff, I think, and even though I yell "BLERGH" at my parents when they watch mooshy movies for the two hundredth time, I do think I get it now. It is beautiful, really. And yet part of me is scared. Am I stupid and boring? Don't I long for my own personal paragon of masculinity to grab me and hold me tightly and neverneverneverever let me go? Ask me in two years.

Afterthought: I mentioned that weird feeling in my tummy to Granny Ed, about my friendship with Iphis. She laughed at me and said I had fallen in love with my best friend. I got all annoyed and told her she was being ridiculous. She prodded me with the tofu on the end of her fork and said it was NO BIG DEAL. I shouldn't be freaked out even if I had. Who cares? She shrugged and pushed her silver hair behind one ear with her knife (!!!). People fall in love with people they admire all the time, she said. Doesn't matter if they are a man or a woman or alive or dead, speak the same language or are on another continent. I am horribly cursed with a liberal grandmother . . . but she made me feel better. At least, I don't need to mention it to

Mom now. Or Dad. Even worse.

Here's something interesting: Writing by hand is so slow that it slows my mind down, too. I can't hit delete or backspace. My thoughts are permanent. And it's quiet. No clicking keys, just the gentle sound of my hand on the paper and the turning page. These letters are formed by my own hands. I watch the ink coming out of the pen. I enjoy the feel of the smooth ballpoint on the page. I'm using a cheap notebook for my journal, nothing fancy. Didn't want to get anything too precious in case the thoughts I leave inside it are less valuable than the covers. In case the notebook is ashamed of its contents.

FRIDAY

Oh my. I've been lost in a good book many times, but this time I'm lost in a really dreadful book. And not in a good way. The book should've come with bread crumbs so I could leave a trail behind me. The main character is so dull. TWO boys are chasing her, and she is miserable. TWO? Am I supposed to feel sorry for this person?

I'm over halfway through the book, and I still don't know what this person really wants. Suddenly, reading feels like homework. Is it wrong to return a library book without finishing it? I need something else to read. It's almost an emergency because the book was really long so I didn't follow my usual habit of getting two books at once. I have no backup! I'm stuck! Calm down, Thisbe. You will get another book soon. Breathe.

RANDOM THOUGHT: I think I prefer reading books to reading online. Library books smell so much better.

Have been reading over my journal again, having tossed that dreadful book on my floor. I think this Era of Weirdness must also have something to do with that stupid belly button-piercing episode. It was a few months ago. We were all at the mall together (what fun) when Melinda and Kel announced that they had a "private thing" to do. Something about an errand for Kel's mom. I went off and poked about in the bookstore for a while, then went back to the food court at the arranged time. What do you know? Melinda and Kel arrived slightly late and giggling madly. They had some great and terrible secret, and they were both really flushed.

It took me about four and a half seconds to figure out that they'd both had their belly buttons pierced: they were scratching their stomachs like they'd both caught fleas. They must have known that I wouldn't be into it, or thought that I would tell Melinda's mom, who would have kittens if she found out. I am not stupid. I wasn't going to tell ANYONE'S mom, even mine. I wasn't sure how I felt at the time. Left out, I guess. As though they didn't trust me. Melinda lifted up her shirt to show me the wound on her belly (which I was afraid would turn nasty) and made a dumb joke about it getting in the way of my Speedo; she only ever wears a bikini, of course. Hmph. I don't know if she's right. I'm not going to pierce my belly button to find out.

I think that's when the friend trouble really started. But the trouble rose from there. And it's come to a peak with our Audience assignment, which, overall, I would have to say is educationally excellent. I love feeling free to do what I want. Speaking of freedom, I think it has liberated me from a couple of stale friendships. What do you know? Freedom has no limits. Hmm. Some other personal observations on Mr. Oliver's approach to teaching:

1. "Authentic" assignments mean that he only has to design one handout; we do all the work!

2. MY COVER IS BLOWN! If I have to be Real and Authentic all the time, people will find out how much I enjoy English class, and I will never be able to fake it again. RATS.

Back to the real purpose of my journal entry: my day at school. Today, we had a Careers class, where we were given an assignment called "All about me." This time, it was my heart that sank into my shoes, and stayed there, my shoes and beyond . . . down, down, down, to the fiery bowels of the earth. The idea is that we'll "get to know ourselves." I wonder about this. If I can get to know myself, how many people am I? Or do I mean "are we"? Here's the Authentic Reflective part at the end:

Speak honestly about your personal experience. Give an example of a situation that you could have handled differently and illustrate how your personality type affected your reactions to this situation.

I've done Gran's questionnaire already, so in theory, I now know myself (or one of my selves) really well. Like the back of my own hand, which I haven't examined carefully in years. *peers closely at hand* WAIT! Where did that scar come from???

Sigh. I have two weeks to complete this assignment, and my response is supposed to be "sincere." Quelle horreur! (I'm sincerely glad this one isn't collaborative.) It's like being told to write a journal reflection by a teacher and then having to hand it in. As if I would EVER show my journal to anyone. Or like opening your closet and finding someone you barely know in there, looking back at you.

SATURDAY

I am an introvert, so let's see how my Careers teacher evaluates this Authentic SILENCE

SUNDAY

But wait! All I have to do is go back to Gran's questionnaire and do it again, pretending that I am the lovely Gwendolyne La Bon-Bon (or maybe I should do it as Fishbone?!). I can answer the questions as HER/HIM, make my assignment all pretty, stick some twinkly butterfly stickers on it, and I'm done! It may sound like lying, but here's my defense: it's good Novelist Training (see, I take my future career seriously; this is what my father would laughingly call "professional development"). It's not LYING. It's FICTION.

So there you have it. Ta-da! A⁺, pretty, AND authentic . . . for someone other than me. Here I go: pen at the ready and all set to fake it. No, not faking it. I'm telling the truth about one of the possible versions of me that I might bring to school on any given day.

I asked Granny Ed, just to be sure. She said that lying and "packaging the truth" weren't the same thing at all. Then she sat on my bed and practically dictated the assignment to me. Wow, I think she reads teachers' minds. I'm convinced she gave me EXACTLY what Ms. Chambers wanted. She'll never guess. It'll sound so Authentic and Sincere that she'll believe she gave us the perfect assignment.

I love my grandmother! This is way bigger than the Great Dishwasher Disaster. This saved my dignity, although I am beginning to think that my grandmother IS Gwendolyne La Bon-Bon.

PS We left out the part about "extreme trouble mating." We didn't think you had to be THAT Authentic.

PPS Granny Ed swatted away my guilty feelings about that dreadful book I abandoned. She said that life was too short to waste on bad reading . . . so we walked to the library this evening and shoved the miserable thing through the return slot. I think even Chutney was happy to see it go.

Week Seven, May 14

MONDAY

Since the library was closed last night, I haven't had a chance to borrow a new book. Maybe I can reread an old favorite? Let's see: maybe I should read another "teen" novel? But no boys chasing girls. Something contemporary, gritty, and challenging? Or maybe it will be a touching and insightful portrayal of adolescence in urban Vancouver?

RANDOM THOUGHT: I am struck with the terrible possibility that I AM a teen novel.

This is no good at all. I need to be something else. Maybe a historical drama, so that I can wear big dresses? No. I should be a fantasy novel, battling demons and scoundrels with an enchanted sword. Or maybe I could be Gwendolyne, instead of Granny Ed?

Thisbe's Kingdom

The mathematical symbols on Thisbe's purple robe glowed brightly. Equilateral triangles, circles, and signs of all kinds flashed as she swept toward her enemy. Her sword, the mystical Eeb Na Foofoo, showered math-flavored sparks as it sliced through the air, declaring its sacred heritage with every swoop. An enchanted alloy of iron, troll gold, and wild black-currant jelly, crafted by the famous sword-making trolls of Dzaki, this sword was indestructible. Whoever tamed the wild black currants at its heart would be mistress of all she surveyed, an empress in a kingdom of silent, fearful subjects.

Such an empress was Thisbe. There was no need for her tremendous displays of power, but she was a bit of a drama queen and rather enjoyed the flashing eyes and twirling swords that came with the whole evil-sorceress package. The unfortunate thing was that, while Thisbe was possessed by all manner of evil spirits, she did not possess an extraordinarily commanding voice. No matter how much she practiced in front of her bathroom mirror, she could not muster anything more threatening than a soft, little squeak. So she settled for growling at her foes (who trembled in their slippers) and trying to convey her meaning with an extraordinary range of facial expressions.

Fortunately Thisbe and her dragon, Pearl, were telepathic, so she never had to utter any orders aloud. She simply thought them and the graceful, impressive creature was ready for takeoff. (Truth be told, their working relationship was a little strained, but a good takeoff never failed to impress the peasants.) Pearl watched Thisbe swing Eeb Na Foofoo over her head. Her arms were getting tired, and the sharp blade was flying perilously close to her own extremities. Thisbe's nose, in particular, was in grave danger. Pearl munched quietly on some dried lizards, wondering how long this would continue. Nobody could seethe with rage, brimful of deadly curses, for long, without a foe to slice. A warrior's motivation was bound to start drooping.

As Pearl picked the bones from her teeth and threw the lizard wrapper in the recycling pile, the dragon thought it might be time for a career change. She was bored with the nine to five. Those few battles with Thisbe's greatest foe, Tarragon Vinegar, were pretty predictable. They always ended the same way: with two survivors. Pearl hoped that Thisbe was too busy to read her mind at that moment.

"Arrrrrggghghhhhhhh!!!!!!!!!!!!!!" Thisbe dropped Eeb Na Foofoo on the sandy floor of her cave. Too bored to watch anymore, Pearl turned around; so that when Thisbe looked at the dragon, she could see no more than Pearl's fabulously scaly tail and her enormous, nay towering, behind. By the time Thisbe caught her breath, Peal had already sent an email to Lady Gwendolyne La Bon-Bon, who was advertising for new staff. . . .

....

....

175

Hmm. I don't think I have the upper-body strength to be a fantasy heroine. So let's see . . .

"Am I <u>Really</u> a Young Adult Novel?"
By Thisbe

Does anyone bully me? Not as badly as some people I know. Do I love someone who doesn't love me back? No. My parents are healthy. They love me. None of my friends have died. I LOVE food. My skin is fine. Mostly.

My cat thinks I'm the greatest can opener ever to walk the earth. My granny doesn't think I'm totally ridiculous. I don't pine for boys. I want to be left alone so that I can READ.

And the big one: I don't spend my time wishing that I could join the in-crowd. In fact, I just escaped it and I feel GREAT!!

Is this what people call "counting your blessings"? I have read a <u>ton</u> of online book reviews now and have decided that I want to be:

Exuberant
Engaging
Striking
Original
Refreshing
Intelligent

But I do not want to be:
    Poignant (now that I've looked it up)
    Touching
    Moving
    Contemporary
    Challenging

Conclusion: My life is not even as interesting as a teen novel. If I could be picturesquely (another new word), lyrically (one of my dad's words) MISERABLE, I might be ok. Clearly, I need to work on this. Perhaps my search will reveal that I am a modern adaptation of an ancient myth, as my name would suggest. I can only dream.

TUESDAY

I'm getting nothing done, and it's my turn to write to Iphis. Or rather, nothing apart from a poem about how I am getting nothing done.

        The Procrastinator
        Got up at 10,
        Wrote a line or two.
        Now it's 3pm
        And I'm emailing them to you.

        You've heard of the Bionic Man,

Wonder Woman and
The Terminator,
Robocop and Batman, well . . .
I'm the Procrastinator.

A title came to me in
The shower so
I went for a walk
To think about it
For an HOUR.
The words wouldn't come
So I made some toast and
Tried to remember a
Tune I could hum:
Tum, tum, tiddly um.

You've heard of the Bionic Man,
Wonder Woman and
The Terminator,
Robocop and Batman, well . . .
I'm the Procrastinator.

And is this poem finished?
Nah, I'll finish it later.

Wrote some emails to Mom and Dad. They wrote almost

every day last week, and I think I ignored them. Oops. This week they have been staying with Dad's oldest sister in Brighton. I remember seeing her when I was there, too, when I was about eight. Her hair was shaped like a big ball, and she'd have these huge parties in the winter. She'd kiss me and I'd come away smelling of her perfume. I always wanted to hurry upstairs to wash it off. Mom and Dad must be having fun, taking "bracing" walks along that pebbly beach.

They are spending this week with tons of people I can't remember, but who seem to know everything about me. They were telling me about a meal they had, where Dad wanted to photograph the dessert for me but was prevented from doing so by the restaurant staff. They thought he was a cake spy (!!). He told me he'd settle for "painting a picture with words instead." I must admit, the dessert sounded pretty fantastic. I'm pleased to report that his email did NOT rhyme. At last!

WEDNESDAY

I tried a little experiment. It was Fishbone's idea. He loves to poke fun at the games people play. He is actually quite manipulative. Last night he sat there twitching his long, whiskery eyebrows, and somehow I understood what he meant for me to do. He is a subtle commander. I put down my Careers assignment, which is becoming more beautiful and less TRUE by the minute, and dragged Granny Ed away from _CSI_. We went to the late-night pharmacy (I love that store) and bought some 99-cent eye shadow. It was a very pale, sparkly green.

Here's my thinking: Melinda loves to be looked at . . . and people do just what she wants. They look at her. I don't want people to notice me. And that works, too. I am Chameleon Girl. So why not change camps for the day?

This morning, I put on some of the eye shadow. It was quite subtle, so Granny Ed helped me cake on a bit more. Then I grabbed an old gloopy mascara of my mom's. That did the trick. I had enormous eyelashes like black tentacles (I pulled the gloopy bits off) and shiny, sparkly eyelids. Then I gooped my hair. Perfect. Even Fishbone was impressed by my disguise.

Then I went to school as usual, saying hi to the same people, stepping around Lovestruck Puppy Melinda and Her Human Popsicle. I went to my locker, and while I was digging around in there, Kel and _her_ Popsicle showed up. As my gran would say, it was smashing. What a moment. Melinda shut her locker door and saw me innocently standing there. WELL. I'm not sure how to describe her face. It was if a Nice spell had been cast on her. She asked what brand of eye shadow I was wearing. Of COURSE I didn't tell her it was 99 cents and that my grandmother helped me pick it. Or that I had tried on so many colors that my hand looked like a tropical fish. I pretended that it was an expensive European brand my mom had sent over.

If only I'd had a secret camera with me today. I even went into the cafeteria! Melinda and Kel ate lunch with me, at "their" table. They talked to me for more than five minutes, and we even laughed about that Bodies in Motion assignment for PE. From the outside, we looked like three of the best pals in the world. On the inside, I was laughing my PANTS off.

I tried to walk like they do, imagining that instead of my bird's-nest hair, I had Kel's impossibly shiny curtain of chestnut-brown locks. I have never figured out how her hair is so shiny: when she moves, her whole hairdo moves, like liquid, not like hair. She is like an animated heroine brought to life. That's how I pictured myself as I sashayed into the lineup for a plateful of carbohydrates (with a side of carbs). I stood there looking fashionably bored. I even noticed that some of the boys who wear those white sports jerseys were looking at me, which normally I would hate (if it ever happened) but today, it was a different look. It was a triumph! It was perfect. No, it was SUBLIME!

Or it was, until David came looking for me, after lunch. He tugged his headphones off, leaned toward me and whispered, "I'm onto you!"

I froze. RATS. I thought I had everyone fooled. "What?" I said, batting my iridescent eyelids at him.

"This is irony, right?" he continued.

"I'm not sure I understand. . . ."

"Don't give me that!" he said, and poked me with his pencil. "It's a big joke, isn't it? You're not really one of those chickies, are you? Don't tell me I had you wrong all this time!" He stared at me as if I had something strange growing out of the top of my head.

Then I crumbled. I confessed that yes, this was indeed a big joke and there would be only one performance of my strange sideshow. He was very relieved. He made me promise to go home and wash the makeup off after school. But I didn't reveal the name of my co-conspirator. I protected Fishy, even under the enormous pressure of interrogation. I would make an excellent spy.

And now that I know what it's like to be one of those girls, I don't have to do it again. . . .

THURSDAY

Today David and I hung out in the computer lab at lunchtime. The fonts in my PE presentation have rebelled against me! They're all different sizes and they're all over the place. Watching the whole presentation from beginning to end is enough to make you go cross-eyed. David's fixing it for me. It already looks much tidier and more professional, rather than something a six-year-old would dream up. Now my words appear gracefully, instead of bouncing and flashing.

But it's not all one-sided. I'm fixing the run-on sentences in his English project and have given him a huge list of adjectives, with the challenge to use as many as he can. It seemed so dry, which is a pity when he cares so much about the subject. It's so lovely to hear him talk about his grandpa in private. I wanted his assignment to flow as gently and easily as his words do when he's explaining an exercise about triangles. . . .

David stopped to stretch and looked over at my hands. "Are you sure you aren't an android or something? You type unnaturally fast." I stopped typing and didn't know what to say. So I changed the subject.

"Do you date?" How's that for creating a diversion?

"Excuse me? Like . . . girls?" he replied, sounding flustered.

"No. Marsupials! Sure, girls. Boys. Whatever, you know."

"Hmm. Interesting question. No, I don't. Not at all. You?"

"Have you seen the boys at this school? Ugh. Sorry, I didn't mean ugh at you. Just I don't think of you in that way. Oh, sorry. What did I say? You're my friend, right?" I was blushing, mumbling, and backpedaling as fast as I could. Which I'm not good at. I'm not even that good at pedaling forward.

"I do know. And it's ok. I don't need you to think about me in that way. I'm kind of busy, with my grandpa and all. I don't think I need to date at the moment."

"It's nice to hear you say that. Coming from a boy. I thought everyone dated except me." By now my face was coming back to its normal color. Not purple, in other words.

"You aren't the only one, Fiz. Trust me!" He looked right at me, pushing his glasses up his nose. "I don't know what your friends tell you, but . . ."

"Oh no!" I had to interrupt him. "They aren't really my friends anymore. If you mean Melinda and Kel, that is. They hardly talk to me." (Of course, I didn't say "Melinda and Kel" to David, because he knows them by their real names.)

"That's harsh!" David looked at me closely. I could see him checking up on me, to see how I really was. I guess he got into the habit of checking on people with his grandpa. I could tell that he was wondering, Is she angry? Is she sad? If I really _were_ a teen novel, I should be angry and sad in bucket loads. I thought for a minute.

"You know what? I think I'm actually ok. I have known them for a long time, but I have new friends, like you. And Iphis, of course."

"When do I get to meet this Iphis?" asked David.

"You don't . . . or at least, not until I have. I haven't met her in person yet."

"Never?" he asked me. By then he'd completely forgotten about rescuing my PowerPoint presentation.

"No. She's my online friend, remember? Um . . . do you think that's really weird?"

"Not really. I have online friends that I've known for years. We play games together all the time. I don't think I'll ever meet them." He paused. "On the other hand, one of them lives in Arizona and the other one's in Illinois." David went back to his typing, stabbing at the keys and staring at his hands. Some older boys had come into the lab and sat down a couple of rows ahead of us. He didn't want to keep talking while they were in earshot, I could tell.

A few minutes later, I looked up from David's Audience Assignment and caught sight of the computer screens at the front of the room. I tapped David on the shoulder and pointed to the boys ahead of us. Barely restraining myself from snorting with laughter, I typed "They are looking at SWIMSUIT models!!!!" David's eyes got big and round. I deleted it and went back to my work, trying not to laugh. David leaned to one side as the boy in front closed a browser window showing a girl in an orange bikini. David grinned. I think it was the biggest grin I've ever seen on anyone. His teeth were practically gleaming. I opened up a new text file and typed "TOUGH GUYS NOT SO TUFF!!! Tuff guys desperate and pathetic in fact, ha ha ha . . ." Snorting quietly, I highlighted my last note, hit delete, and began to write a poem:

> YOU may look TOUGH but
> Your clothes still smell of
> YOUR MOMMY'S fabric softener.

It was supposed to be a haiku. I know it didn't end up as one, but it was worth writing it just for the grin on David's face.

FRIDAY

Had an AMAZING dream last night. I was giving a performance of a poem I had written. It was the most incredible bit of writing. Every single word was perfect. I used words I never thought I would use. Words I didn't even think I knew!

Woke up feeling really, really proud . . . until I realized

that I couldn't remember a single word of my masterpiece. Gone! The whole thing.

But I FINALLY finished that medieval story about Gwendolyne La Bon-Bon. I was finding it really hard to stay motivated so I pasted my latest bit into an email to Mom and Dad and then just kept typing. The end of the story is very sarcastic. I thought my dad would laugh at it. Somehow the thought of him and Uncle Al snorting over it made me keep going. I just typed and typed and before I knew it, I was done. Does that count as "writing," when it was really just an email? Or do I need to be stuck away in my tower, writing in complete isolation? Somehow it feels like cheating! I'll get over it, though. Especially when I am a famous author with a page-full of books, ha . . .

SATURDAY

From: Thisbe
To: Iphis
Subject: weirdness

Something is weird over here. Something feels different. Something in my daily life. I am still going to school, of course, but I don't feel as though I am there. Maybe it's because my folks have been away for so long? Somehow I feel invisible. I feel as though I am in a dream or a bubble or something.

When I'm not sitting at a lunch table with a pen in my hand or at the computer, I'm still thinking about it—thinking about writing stuff and sending it to you, getting on with the assignment, and all the billion other things that are coming out. Am I sick? Is this what obsessions are? Should I worry? Right now I think more about our friendship than I do about the friends I supposedly have at Johnson—and I've known them, in person, in the flesh, for years.

At lunchtime yesterday, the girls asked if I'd come along for pizza. I had my lunch with me but didn't want them to think that this was an Eating Thing. I am sure they are convinced that I haven't eaten since January. I haven't gone out for lunch with them in weeks now, and I feel like an outcast. But that's nothing new.

So there I am in the lab at lunchtime, working away studiously on my assignment, and I'm thinking . . . about this assignment. What kind of Audience assignment will it be? I have some stories, some comments, an Audience, some emails . . . so what? Great ingredients, Thisbe, but I need a whole cake. Or a packet mix. At any rate, I know that this is much more than an assignment. It's a statement. It's my life mission. I wish my words would stop scowling at me. I can't finish them. I don't want to. I don't know how.

Why do I write? These words are my world, my empire, my kingdom. They are my turf, my territory, and my subjects. While relationships with people are flawed and have seasons like the earth, words can germinate, grow, blossom, give fruit, shrivel, and scatter in people's minds throughout the course of their lives. . . . Words are eternal but ever changing. They leave something behind. They do not die.

That last part might be a quote from Milton. My dad has it on a sticky note in his office. Dad doesn't usually quote his own writing on sticky notes, but there's a first time for everything. . . .

Where do stories live once we have written them down? Are they still stuck to us, the people who wrote them, living and breathing in time with us?

No. They are separate, living a life of their own. They can march off into a store, withdraw books on my precious library card, grab a coffee with some nouns and adjectives, do all kinds of normal human-type stuff (like sending emails full of horrible grammar or apologizing over and over to people who hadn't noticed you were grouchy) . . . WITHOUT ME!

I _must_ learn to send my words into the world to live a separate life. A separate existence. I just bring them into the world, and then I have to let them run. I hope they come home and tell me what happened, how they ended and if they ended. . . .

At the moment, they don't seem to end; that's the problem. There are just more words. And the old ones get older and then they sit, glowering at me from the corners, not wanting to leave. I can't keep holding their hands! I have to hand them in to Mr. Oliver! But I don't want to finish them. They are mine! If I let them go, they would get older without me. I don't mind coddling them for now, wiping their typos and burping them when they're full of hot air, but these babies must be free, free, free! I should want them to ride off and get muddy. I always wanted to show my writing to other people, but now I am afraid to. . . .

Hmm. I like that. I'm going to send it to Iphis, for our assignment, from "Where do stories live" to "afraid to."

From: Iphis
To: Thisbe
Subject: getting old
Thisbe, I feel the same. I don't think you are obsessed. I think you

are an amazing writer. And trust me. Your words will get old without you. They already sound old. Are you sure you are only in 9th grade?

From: Thisbe
To: Iphis
Subject: Re: getting old
You are way too nice to me. Even my grandmother isn't that nice to me and she loves me. Do I need to pay for these services, or are they free of charge?

From: Iphis
To: Thisbe
Subject: Re: Re: getting old
Just pay me with more of your words.

From: Thisbe
To: Iphis
Subject: *hugs Iphis firmly*
Welcome to my kingdom.

SUNDAY
From: Iphis
To: Thisbe
Subject: *claps hands sharply* To business!
The committee (Fishy and I) have decided that you need to relax (we conferred earlier; don't panic, he didn't tell me anything I didn't already know. About you, that is. . . . About everything else . . . well, that was some interesting conversation).

Here 'tis: You need some light relief! Here's my Put-the-Fizz (geddit?) back-into-your-life program. It's a little Flash quiz I found. It's a test to see if you are a geek. Take it, go on!

From: Thisbe
To: Iphis
Subject: Re: *claps hands sharply* To business!
I will try it . . . but I see that you don't have to. You found it, babe. That's the ultimate test! Should I worry? Should I check in with my parents? Should I write to an agony column?

From: Iphis
To: Thisbe
Subject: business
Nope! But you could make me an iron-on T-shirt that says GEEK on it in shiny silver letters.

Week Eight, May 21

MONDAY

From: Iphis
To: Thisbe
Subject: a new gift for Thisbe

Hey! I drew another picture of you . . . but this time I was serious. See, you are now Thisbe the Warrior, brandishing your favorite weapon: the PEN!! Mightier than the sword, right? How do you like the super-heroine suit?

From: Thisbe
To: Iphis
Subject: nice suit

Hmm . . . it's . . . dashing? Not sure if it's really me, though. Bit on the slinky side. The pens in my hair are nice (wait, did I get it chopped since my mermaid days?). What did I do to my face? Seems as though I cut myself on my sharp wits, ha ha ha. . . .

Pardon me, milady. I must be off now. Have urgent appointment to spread terror in kingdom.

TUESDAY

Suddenly I can write again without all my thoughts getting in the way.

I've put my pen down and am back at the keyboard to keep up with the pace of my thoughts. I'm sitting at my desk, typing away in a frenzy, a passion. I don't look at my fingers. I am like a pianist, playing with my eyes closed. Occasionally I open my eyes and look at the screen. My eyes dart back and forth repeatedly, reading and rereading the last sentences I have written. It doesn't feel like writing. I am not really using my brain. It's using me. Or someone or something is. I am in space. I reach for the soda can balanced on the pile of books by the printer. I drain out the last dregs, suck them down, read once more, sling the can at the garbage—don't watch to see if it goes in. My aim is terrible. Really terrible. I look. There's a sticky drip running down the side of the wall. Oh well.

I lean back in my chair. I reach my arms above my head and hear my shoulders crack. Take some deep breaths. It's ok. It's not bad. I am happy. My words are gone, quietly swimming through my computer's hard drive, down the wires, into the soda-stained wall; like a swarm of bees, they chase one another, noun after noun after adjective and preposition and dangling participle, racing ahead of the others. . . . They chase around the electrical sparks into the bones of my house, through telephone lines, server upon server . . . until someone, somewhere, turns on, boots up . . . and reads. I wonder if it'll be Iphis.

But nothing from Iphis today.

My Haiku from Spam Titles
Giraffe stenographer
Oppose liquid glib
Profundity approvals

WEDNESDAY

From: Thisbe
To: Iphis
Subject: where are you?

Where have you been?? I'm getting nervous. We don't have long, and we haven't really done the assignment yet. And aren't you going to send me a picture? I just sent you one from my private email address, thisbe668@gmail.com. I know we're not supposed to . . . but it seemed a bit weird, after eight weeks and writing almost every day. Are you afraid or something? Don't worry! My feet are really weird. I'll send you a picture of them, too, if that would convince you. I need to see how wrong my mental picture is.

From: Iphis
To: Thisbe
Subject: Re: where are you?
Weird feet. *grimaces* Eeeuuuww. Um. Ah. Maybe I'll send you a picture of my feet. My feet are ok.

From: Iphis
To: Thisbe
Subject: Ear you are
five minutes later, after Thisbe's email arrives Ok. Here you go. A picture of me. Am I cute or what?

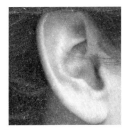

From: Thisbe
To: Iphis
Subject: you?
WHAT is right. WHAT?!!!? A picture of your ear?? Doesn't tell me a thing, girlfriend. Except . . . your ears aren't pierced. I always pictured you with a few perforations. Or maybe they aren't in your ears?

From: Iphis
To: Thisbe
Subject: Hey! You sound ear-ritated
Ears, oh yeah—I'm not really the piercing kind. . . . Nope, no

other perforations. Afraid I would sink if I swam. . . .

From: Thisbe
To: Iphis
Subject: More, please!
Well?

Kel teased me today about my imaginary friend. She was trying to be bold like Melinda. I told her that not seeing Iphis in person, in her body, made no difference to me. Had she heard of the expression "kindred SPIRIT"? Didn't it suggest that you could be kin even if you weren't there in body? She didn't know what I was talking about. . . . Having no body would be AWFUL for Kel and Melinda. I am sure they couldn't imagine it.

This could be the problem: My ex-friends aren't writers. Even David isn't a writer. Does that matter? Should I be hanging out with people who are like me? Should I start by hanging out with people who LIKE me?

RANDOM THOUGHT: Is there room on Planet Earth for all the storytellers who want to inhabit it, or do some people have to give up on their writing?

The other problem with being a writer is that you have to really like being alone. Sort of makes it hard to meet those kindred spirits. . . . Iphis is a writer, but she is a bit shy about her work. I've hardly seen anything she's written, if you don't include the millions of emails she's sent.

In any case (and in spite of what I said to Kel), I really would like to sit down with Iphis and all our piles of writing . . . grab a soda . . . rustle through them until one of us says "Ooh, this bit is good. Wait, listen to this. I think it's going somewhere. . . ." I dream of having a friend like that. I could ask my parents to help me that way, but I don't want to. After all, they've published a ton of books already and would probably go into teacher-mode. I'd rather sit around and muse about it . . . with my muse. I don't want someone correcting my punctuation. I want someone to meet my ideas and get excited about them. No, parents definitely aren't the right people to confide in about this.

What about teachers? Hmm. My school journals don't count. They aren't real writing. They aren't about being sincere, in spite of what they say. They are about figuring out which bit of critical thinking/learning outcome you're supposed to have and then pretending that—POOF!—as if by magic, you just happened upon your intellectual growth, when the teachers knew all along what they wanted from you.

Ugh. I just read that last paragraph and I'd better stop. I'm beginning to sound like my dad. How unoriginal of me. Must go downstairs and microwave more of Granny Ed's frozen lasagna.

THURSDAY

....

FRIDAY

I'm exhausted today. Haven't heard from Iphis. Maybe I shouldn't have sent her my picture. Maybe she does think I look weird?? That was breaking the rules; I know it. I feel guilty. I hope the picture didn't change what she thought of me. Maybe I'm not the me she expected? Help.

What the heck is this assignment supposed to be, anyway? We have only a few more weeks, and I still have no idea what we are going to hand in. Melinda and Kel don't know, either, but they couldn't care less . . . so I can't ask them.

I have been going over the same ideas in my mind. Yesterday I thought and thought, and now my brain feels like a soggy rag. Thank goodness for Granny Ed. Today she made a special dinner for me. I could have cried. I nearly did when I realized that she had left Chutney with Norm, to cheer him up. He is so smelly at the moment. I mean Chutney, of course—I've never met Norm and am sure he doesn't smell.

Anyhow, the stew had noodles and potatoes and celery in it. Delicious carbs! She called it "chicken soup," but then she reassured me that it was still vegetarian. What she actually said was "No chickens were hurt in the production of this dinner."

I felt, as they say in novels, "quite restored." *pauses to swoon delicately, one hand raised to forehead*

After eating, we went for a brisk Chutney-free walk. On the way home she suggested that since the dog wasn't there, and it was a warm evening, we should go for a swim. I wasn't even aware that she had packed her swimsuit. She hadn't. She said she didn't need one. She would swim in her bra and underwear—who'd know? Me, that's who! EMBARRASSING.

But, she is seventy, so I suppose she had a point. None of the hot young men would be staring at her, so why should she care? There I was, feeling like a tub of butter and she was proud of herself . . . and she really wanted to swim. So we did. Mostly we floated and chatted—like Melinda and Kel do when they go swimming—and she seemed about twenty-five, weightless, beautiful, with her soft, curly hair drifting about her like silver seaweed. It was amazing . . . and nobody noticed that she was in her underwear. Or if they did notice, they didn't care. I love this city.

But here is the best bit:
We got out of the pool after about half an hour, and as we wandered toward the changing rooms, I realized that she was heading in the wrong direction. She was heading swiftly for the MEN'S changing room. She's pretty shortsighted and my reactions were a bit slow, so I had to make a lunge for her and take her arm (not too hard, I hope—her arms are tiny) and say, "Not that way, Gran! That's for boys!" Of

course I was right under the lifeguard's chair. Granny Ed wasn't flustered in the slightest. She just lifted up her little chin and kept taking her little bird steps, looked up at the handsome, blond lifeguard in the chair, smiled, and said "You don't know—maybe I meant to go there!" I have to admit, she's pretty funny. I'm beginning to appreciate my dad's sense of humor. He is such a goof, too.

I wish Mom and Dad would come home sooner. Or do I? Things are going pretty well with Gran, in spite of my early efforts to sabotage her stay. My parents' plot has worked, i.e., shut us in the same house together for twelve weeks and eventually peace is declared between all species. . . . I can't help wondering: would we have conversations like this if Grandpa Michael were here? Of course, I'm still sad about losing him but perhaps I have gained something, too?

On the bus, I told Ed that I was worried about my assignment and Iphis (I didn't mention that I had sent her my photo). Granny Ed said that I shouldn't be such a *English moment approaching* "fusspot." Iphis was just fine, but she had another life, a REAL one (which annoyed me), and there were plenty of people in it that can take care of her. I told her I AM REAL, TOO, YOU KNOW. She just smiled.

She also said that she'd never met an Iphis before. She wondered where the name came from—I told her it sounded Greek, but then I realized that I didn't know.

Still haven't heard from Iphis. My assignment could be doomed. That's just typical for "group" projects. But my friend has vanished, too. What am I going to do? I can't believe I'll fail the Assignment. Mom and Dad get back in less than four weeks. At least the house is tidy, and I remembered to feed Fishbone. Wait . . . let me check. Ok. He's still breathing.

I should be glad that my parents aren't obsessed with the idea of failure. It's like it doesn't even occur to them that I'm anything but responsible. Sometimes, I wish my parents didn't trust me so completely. I wish they would jump up and down about the 84% I just got on a French test. But they won't, because they aren't experiencing the same feeling of relief that I am. They didn't see my panicking, my face burning and prickling in class when I got the test back, sure that I had failed.

What if did screw up, just this once? Would they even know what to say? I hope not. My face is burning again, just thinking about it. Maybe this whole experience will be like that French test. Maybe I will get 84% for this, too.

SATURDAY

Where is Iphis? Has she given up, gone away, or suffered some terrible calamity? I will need to speak to Mr. Oliver soon. I don't know her last name so I can't look her up in the phone book—I'm not supposed to, anyway. Hmm. All you need is the Web, right? Granny got me thinking. Who is Iphis??

<u>Later that day:</u>

I can't think straight. My mind is a mess. I will write down what happened and hope it makes sense afterward. I'm watching my hands as I type. They shake . . .

First, I edged forward on my chair and reached for the mouse. At that moment, Fishbone, who had just woken up from a marathon nap, realized that I had turned my attention to my keyboard. With none of his usual feline grace, he leapt from the bed onto the desk, landing with one paw on a broken pencil that I had been meaning to throw away. The pencil skittered across the desk onto the floor as Fishbone prepared to lay his full bulk on the keys.

I grabbed Fishbone around the tummy and lifted him gently off the keyboard onto the bed, where he meowed indignantly for a second before turning in circles to renew his nest.

(See how I'm taking my time here? I'm letting my thoughts collect themselves. . . . I hope they do a good job on their own, because I lost track of them completely about an hour ago. Leave them alone and they'll come home. . . .)

I opened my browser and let my thoughts drift. Key words wandered in and out of my head. I typed in "Iphis" and "Vancouver" and waited. Results 1 to 10 of 23. I scrolled down, hoping to see Westerley High School. I looked for photo albums. I looked for poems. I looked for basketball teams. I looked for anime clubs. I looked for anything that would suggest a tall young woman with class, a bright smile and an independent mind, a sense of humor and a love of wordplay.

Nothing. Nothing but a bunch of music sites, something in French, something in—what was that? Greek?—a cruise Web site, male baby names. Ok, tried again.

Westerley High School. There was the site, but no Iphis. "Sports at Westerley." Girls' Basketball. No Iphis.

I told Granny Ed what I was doing. She said I should be careful. You never know what you might find on the Web. I think she imagines it's all porn and personality tests.

Male baby names seemed weird, but I thought I'd follow up. Fishy thought that sounded ok. I found a philosophy page. A page for name interpretation . . . It told me all about people called "Iphis." "Idealistic" sounded about right. She's also a "peacemaker"—I know that she hated seeing her mom and dad argue. But is she "sensitive and self-conscious"? I didn't know. Maybe I don't know her that well after all. I mean, she sent me a photo of her EAR. "Secretive"? Yo—I thought— that's my girl! Does this person know her or what? Poor thing, having a boy's name. Must be like having the name "Robin" before anyone thought girls should be named after birds. (Or boys.)

But why couldn't I find her on the Westerley site? Maybe she's new? Maybe it's a nickname? She never said anything, and I never thought to ask.

Cr*p. We have to finish this thing soon.

Granny Ed said, "Hey, it's not that weird! I have a boy's name, after all." I told her that her name was really Edna and that everyone knew it—but she had an answer for that, too.... She doesn't say Edna when she writes angry letters to newspaper editors. She thinks she has a better chance of getting her name in the paper as "Ed." My grandmother is a sneak.

But then a terrible thought struck me, as I read pages and pages of Greek mythology, and I couldn't believe what I was seeing: *Secrecy. Male baby names. Greek myths about things that turn into other things* . . . Iphis's love of Greek mythology! Of course! Who calls their daughter IPHIS in Vancouver, in this day and age? (So what if I have a strange name? My parents are academics!) HOW could I be so stupid?

From: Thisbe
To: Iphis
Subject: YOU
I just did a search on your name. Did you plan on telling me who (or rather WHAT) you REALLY were? EVER?

From: Thisbe
To: Iphis
Subject: YOU again
WHAT were you thinking? *Were* you thinking? I don't know what to think. Don't email me.

From: Iphis
To: Thisbe
Subject: me and me again
Sorry. . . .

From: Thisbe
To: Iphis
Subject: too speechless to think of one
Can't you READ? I said DON'T EMAIL ME. You must have laughed your head off at me. Go away.

From: Iphis
To: Thisbe
Subject: speechless
It's not that big a deal—is it? I didn't actually LIE to you. Did you read over our emails? Weren't they real? Did I ever ACTUALLY say that I WASN'T a boy?

From: Iphis
To: Thisbe
Subject: are you there?
Hello?
Hello?

From: Iphis
To: Thisbe
Subject: trying again
Hello?

From: Iphis
To: Thisbe
Subject: and again
Hello-o-o-o-o?
a lonely voice echoes loudly throughout the empty caverns of Thisbe's Kingdom

From: Iphis
To: Thisbe
Subject: Fw: and again
Come back, Thisbe! Please come back!

<u>The code of love: a poem for Thisbe</u>
Shower me with sweet applets,
My love; animate me with
Crisp lines of dulcet code
To which my bounding heart
And tender nerves are owed.

You push my buttons, baby!
I'M ALL IN UPPERCASE!
I miss you! I love you!
I need to see your
Smiling ☺ face!

SUNDAY

From: Iphis
To: Thisbe
Subject: hello
Are you there? I am. I'm waiting.

From: Iphis
To: Thisbe
Subject: joke
Q: What do you call a dinosaur who's up to no good?
A: Dyouthinkhesaurus!

From: Thisbe
To: Iphis
Subject: no, I'm not here
Aren't you going to get a new ID, now that you have a new GENDER?? I have to hand it to you: you picked a name from a myth about a girl . . . who turns into a boy. You were covered both ways. Very clever.

From: Iphis
To: Thisbe
Subject: the new me
Please, Thisbe! Don't hate me. Don't be like Thisbe in the play—talking to her lover through a hole in a wall.

You're killing me! Email is just the tiniest hole in a wall. Please write back. Be Thisbe Version 1.0 again?

From: Thisbe
To: Iphis
Subject: the new YOU? you aren't YOU
Go away. Truth isn't measured out in fractions. You made your choice.

"Thisbe Version 2.0 is the final update. You have erased the previous version. Are you sure you want to shut down now? Yes. What do you want the computer to do? Restart? Shut down? Shut down."

Bye-bye.

I have had thirty-five thoughts today. Maybe thirty-six. My brain feels as though it has a hamster in it, running in a wheel. The wheel is going around and around, squeak, squeak, squeak, squeak . . . I haven't even told Granny Ed yet. Ugh.

But I did ask her what would happen if I wrote a book and there wasn't room for it in the Book World. If there were no space the same shape as my book, waiting to receive it. Granny said that it didn't matter. That I should write my book and see. The other books would move aside and make room for mine.

How does she know these things? She is very wise. Wonder if we'll still have conversations like this after my mom and dad get back?

From: Iphis
To: Thisbe
Subject: doing my best

I've written you a poem and sent you an animated card. I've even drawn a picture of YOU as a Japanese anime heroine . . . the greatest vanquisher of evil!! I've taken a three-day beating from Sienna, who is threatening to move home again because of this. Please write back properly before she does! Can I send you flowers??

In purgatory—Jason.

From: Thisbe
To: Iphis
Subject: when your best isn't good enough

You know I'm not allowed to give out my phone number or address. Rools is rools, baby. SOME PEOPLE LIVE BY THEM.

From: Iphis
To: Thisbe
Subject: Don't shut down . . . restart?

Ow. *slinks away with nose smarting from recent poke*
Can't we start again?

From: Thisbe
To: Iphis
Subject:

Ok. Start again, then. Start with something TRUE.

From: Iphis
To: Thisbe
Subject: Re:
Hello, Thisbe, my name is Jason.

From: Thisbe
To: Iphis
Subject: Re: Re:
SCENE: Audition for role of Best New Girlfriend
Let's give this a try, "Jason." Jasonjasonjasonjasonjason.
Pro: You write well. You're funny. You think I'm funny: this is your best quality.
Con: You are a poor prospect for best new girlfriend because YOU ARE MALE! Your worst quality: you are a LIAR.

Hmm. Now that's a tough one. Sorry, I'm afraid you didn't make it this time, but thanks for trying out and by the way, good luck in your career. I'm sure you will be a great success in your new role as a BOY.

From: Iphis
To: Thisbe
Subject: Re: Re: Re: Re: Re: Re: Re: Re: Re: Re: Re: Re: Re: Re: Re:
We belong together, Fiz. We belong together like bricks and mortar. Like soda cans and wasps. Like cheese and crackers. Like mangoes and dental floss.

From: Thisbe
To: Iphis
Subject: WHAT???

Week Nine, May 28

MONDAY

From: Iphis
To: Thisbe
Subject: this made sense
What's in a name? That which we call a rose
By any other name would smell as sweet.
(*Romeo and Juliet*, II.ii. 46–47)

From: Thisbe
To: Iphis
Subject: not to me
Shakespeare isn't always the answer, jerk. Identity is more than a NAME, you idiot.

And by the way: I did read over our emails and I am still furious. I also looked up "spiced dainties" on the Web. I see that it comes from a poem about a man watching a woman undress, from inside her closet. Nice touch. Classy.

From: Iphis
To: Thisbe
Subject: poem
Well, you found me out. But didn't you LOVE the poem?

From: Thisbe
To: Iphis
Subject: Re: poem

I might have, if I hadn't been too busy being creeped out. Haven't you had that speech about "maturity" from your parents? Didn't you get all that stuff about being honest? Didn't you get the extended remix about how maturity meant telling the TRUTH?

From: Iphis
To: Thisbe
Subject: creep

No. I don't get lectures from either of my parents. They aren't around enough to lecture me. Whoever told you that maturity meant telling the truth? Adults lie ALL the time, or hadn't you noticed?

From: Thisbe
To: Iphis
Subject: adult behavior

Of course. How stupid do you think I am? They are just IMMATURE adults then, aren't they?!

From: Iphis
To: Thisbe
Subject: Re: adult behavior

So what is maturity then, if you're so smart? Adults lie to me all the time. See my father, for example.

From: Thisbe
To: Iphis
Subject: Re: Re: adult behavior
Maturity (from the dictionary of Thisbe)(n): Knowing that sometimes it's ok to lie and sometimes it's not—and being able to tell the difference.

From: Iphis
To: Thisbe
Subject: I'm done here
Well, I'm off. And that's the truth. Bye. Nice knowing you.

From: Thisbe
To: Iphis
Subject: Re: I'm done here
Bye.

Granny Ed is with Thisbe in her bedroom, checking her email. She and Grandpa Michael were going to visit England again before he died. She is glad that her son and his wife can share it together. She is also glad that they are not coming home for three more weeks. Peace may have broken out in Thisbe's home—even between the Cat Zone and Dog Zone—but there is no peace in Thisbe's heart. Not yet.

She can sense the glow of her son's happiness. It comes across loud and clear in his emails—they are long, hilarious, and kind. Ed can tell that Thisbe loves these letters. Timothy and Thisbe seem to get along best now when it's in writing. He's in his element, and she is in her kingdom. It's a world of the utmost respect and affection. They can hug wildly and tell each other stupid secrets here, still.

Ed and Michael used to visit often when Thisbe was a small child. Thisbe was her father's buddy then. They seemed so inseparable. Annabel used to call out their names together, "Timothisbe! Dinner!" when they stayed out in the garden after dark. When Thisbe was four, Annabel went to a conference by herself, and Ed and Michael came up from Seattle. Thisbe woke up in the night, distressed to find that her mother had gone. Timothy had the idea to order pizza at 3:00 am. The delivery guy was expecting a house full of stoned young men with raging appetites. Instead he found an insomniac four-year-old and her tired-looking father and grandparents hoping desperately that a stomach full of carbohydrates would put her to sleep. They all ate the slices in their pajamas on the front steps.

Now, in the same room, the father and daughter each seem to take up more space than a person should. They bump each other with sharp elbows and run chair wheels into each other's ankles. Ed saw it, even in just a few days. Timothy misses his daughter most when he is at home, but he hasn't told anyone about this yet—except his mother. He says he's ok with this, though, most of the time. He knows that she must drift away from him for now. But she should return later on, swimming in a different current.

Right now, Ed can tell her granddaughter's treading water, although she thinks she's sinking steadily. At this point in her life—and even with a steady supply of hugs and lasagna—she can't always tell how well she is doing. She is thinking about her parents, wondering if these weeks would have gone the same way if they had not gone to England. Thisbe feels as though she has failed. The dishwasher was nothing. This is a real disaster.

As they read the emails from Thisbe's parents, Ed has been braiding Thisbe's hair. She is also trying to ignore the wrinkled three-day-old baked potato that's sitting on a saucer, next to Thisbe's keyboard. Ed finishes the braid and tells Thisbe that she doesn't need her help, that she can finish her homework if Fishbone promises to edit the rough copy. Thisbe reassures her that Fishy is nothing if not reliable, and Ed smiles, reaching for the saucer. She leaves the room with the extinct potato, almost closing the door behind her. When she is halfway down the stairs, she hears Thisbe getting out of her chair and climbing onto her bed, where Fishbone is sleeping. She's probably burying her face in Fishbone's fur.

Ed has been watching Thisbe find her feet. It's hard to watch when she seems so lost. Ed can see her looking for her arms and legs, but she wishes Thisbe would find her head and her heart first. In spite of the hours she spends at her computer—she isn't really writing. She's staring at the screen, but the words are hiding from her. They've fled, she says. "Somebody stole them; somebody's dog ate them; they have run away with the monster in the clothes dryer that eats black socks."

Ed comes back upstairs later, and there's Thisbe, still at the *computer. She sits. She stretches. She waits. Nothing. "Why, why, why?" she cries bitterly at her computer screen. "Why do MY words HATE me?" All of her emails to and from Iphis are printed out, in neat piles. Thisbe is too afraid to approach. She circles and circles, hardly getting closer. Ed tells her it is time for all those books she's read to get their revenge. She tells her to give some of her own writing that same tough love. Make it work for its dinner. She even offers to roll up and dog-ear the pages for her. Thisbe looks as though she should be offended, but Ed knows what's really going through her head: "My own writing battered from too much reading. What an amazing thought. . . ."*

Thisbe's determined not to be left speechless in her own kingdom. She almost seems angry now. "No, no, no." She takes a deep breath. The screen blinks back at her blankly, stubbornly. "Some days the words breed on their own, but today—well, they aren't feeling frisky," she says.

Ed tells her that you cannot conquer a kingdom with fear. The pen really IS mightier than the sword. And if this is the case, just imagine what she could do with a keyboard and 80 words per minute? "You can conquer this beast, surely?" Thisbe says that her heart is pounding. That the gap between what she tells herself and what she feels, what she knows to be true, is gigantic. There is a chasm between them, and she cannot leap across that canyon. She turns her screen off, grabs her swimming bag, and heads for the stairs. Ed watches her go and thinks of Timothy. Of how Thisbe is so like him, and how little she knows it.

TUESDAY

Untitled
The pen is mightier
Than the sword.
So Iphis and I fought
A duel with words
And I lost.

It's funny, you know. When you are small, people teach you that opposites are things like black and white, big and small, silly and serious . . .

But I went swimming yesterday and found out something else. After six laps I found that I were into my rhythm. I felt invisible, sleek. I felt as though I were sliding through the topmost molecules of the water. Feeling exhilarated and utterly calm at the same time, my arms and legs perfectly timed, my breathing slow, slow, in, out, as though my mind had gone, and I was just a body, a set of mechanically connected limbs, working with the water. At that moment, a thought fell into my otherwise empty mind: sadness and exercise are opposites as surely as black and white, up and down.

What have I told Jason??????? Did I tell him more than I would tell Mr. Oliver? Definitely. More than my friends. Especially now. More than Granny Ed? Thank goodness I didn't tell everything to Jason, although I definitely thought about it. Way too embarrassing now.

We talked about so much. So much that matters. He's not the person I thought he was. He's a spy, a liar. He was in disguise as a girl. But always Iphis, always in metamorphosis, always knowing that he was becoming a boy.

What does he think of me? I thought I knew what Iphis thought but now—I don't know if boys read and understand the same things that girls do? How can I know what my reader thinks if I can't tell that my reader is who he says he is? Audience, what??

Maybe Audience doesn't matter, after all. If you can never know your Audience (which would be true if I were a real author) you can never write *for* them. You can't assume that they are like you. You must expect them to be different and that they will never truly let you see who they are. Even if they do, they are liable to change halfway through reading your work (and don't you want that, after all?). . . . They might even change from a girl to a boy.

But thank goodness for email. What on EARTH did people do before email? I hate to think. I'd never know what I'd said to people and have to rely on my memory. Or theirs—even worse!

WEDNESDAY

Granny Ed took me to my favorite bakery, conveniently located next to my favorite bookstore. We got a table by the window and sat there talking. Good thing they are open 24 hours. We could have used all of them.

I haven't told my mom about Iphis/Jason yet. Too busy reassuring them what a splendid time I've had with Gran—which is the surprising truth! From their last email, they seem pretty pleased with themselves. Who cares if it was a plot? Now my dad can pull up his huge socks and remind himself what a great person his mom is. I may have made a mess of a few things while they were away, but it was no thanks to Gran. I did that all by myself. . . .

I told Granny Ed everything. Practically melted into a puddle, I was so sad and felt so ashamed and stupid. She could tell that this was serious. Then she said something interesting: We can't help choosing faces for the people we know, and it's natural to be angry because I chose the wrong one, based on who/what I thought Iphis was. That was helpful. She said we all misjudge situations all the time. As I get older I will get into more situations, more of which (laws of probability) I will get wrong. I should get used to being wrong. I didn't find that part so helpful. I had thought my judgment was pretty good.

A comment on the laws of probability: I have also heard that if you were to give a typewriter to 100 monkeys, one of them would eventually write *Romeo and Juliet*. If both events are possible—me being right 100% of the time and a monkey writing Shakespeare—then I have definitely landed on the wrong planet. I hate statistics.

5324521k,sgfsgkjwrasedfaew2781

That was Fishbone, who just walked across my keyboard. Thank you, Fishy. 100 ´monkeys may be able to write Shakespeare, but you are unique.

THURSDAY

. . . .

FRIDAY

We went back to the bakery today, where I proved that it's possible to eat your weight in cheesecake, in less than three days. . . . Granny asked me about my writing and about being online. She's really fascinated by it all.

SATURDAY

This morning Granny Ed made a weird connection. She came into my room while I was hunched over my keyboard, sighed melodramatically, and said I was "still ignoring my body. . . . When would I learn?" Sigh, sigh, etc. etc. Then she flipped her dish towel over her shoulder and folded her arms, looking as though she'd had this big revelation. But she waited to tell me about it until we were back at the bakery today. Actually, she waited until I was tucking into my dessert and wasn't noticing her ingenious interrogation tactics.

"That's why you love writing online? And *being* online? Because you don't have a body when you are writing, when you are in words. You are in your mind, right?" I looked at my shoes. She told me that I can't escape my body forever and that at some point, I might actually like it. She told me to look at myself when I'm hunched over the keyboard. I curl myself into a pretzel when I write, even though I have a great chair (thank you, Mom and Dad). She said that it wasn't enough to spend your life vanishing into your head and into words on a screen. You have to take care of your body, too, because your body and your mind talk to each other. They talk very quietly, so you can't hear them, but if you look after your body, your mind will be nicer to you. Life won't be quite so hard.

I'm not sure I got all of that, and was anxiously smooshing my favorite brownie cheesecake—SO sweet and creamy!— with my fork. That's when she had another of her brilliant ideas. She told me that I was very far from being a "lost cause," because I love swimming. She suggested that I think about different parts of my body when I swim, each time I go. Monday's Feet Day, Tuesday's Knees Day, Wednesday's Thighs Day, and so on. She looked at me very seriously for a moment to let this sink in. Then she said, "And, of course, Sunday's Bum Day." I should have laughed then, but the rhyme was really a long shot.

By that point I must have looked a bit weepy, because she paused for a long time. Then Granny looked down at my destroyed dessert and said, "Oh BOTHER! I knew it. I shouldn't have got you that cheesecake. It's made you cry. But it'll taste good, even if it looks as though it's been run over." Her eyes crinkled, and she put her hand on my wild and woolly hair with such kindness. I don't think I've ever seen her look at me like that. I'm pretty sure *I've* never looked back at her that closely. She smiled, but I thought she was going to cry, too. All she said was, "You're beautiful." It should've been really weird, coming from my grandmother, but it felt like the deepest thing anyone has ever said to me. Wonderful and right and extremely sad and wrong at the same time. A big moment, anyway . . .

And a strange one. My parents will think she has turned me into a different person. They might not be sorry. It's going to be a bit weird to have them back. Great, but weird.

I thought about Granny Ed's homework when I went swimming later. I watched my hands plunging into the water ahead of me at each stroke. "These are my swimming hands," I thought. "And my typing hands. The hands that do what my mind tells them to, my thinking hands. The hands that fill my ideas with ink, make them real. Maybe I was wrong? Maybe bodies *don't* spoil everything after all? These lovely, slightly scarred, sausage-y hands: what would I write without them?"

Down with the pen. Up with the keyboard. My computer screen springs to life.

Mightier Than the Sword
The pen *is* the sword,
The razor and the butter knife.
It is the fish
And the fish in the tide.
It is blood and flowers.
It is smell.
It is thought and time.
It is passage, memory, regret,
Love, hate, sorrow, celebration, and
Finding the
Pair to a lost sock.

It is breath, sickness, forgetting.
It is a sinking ship and the
Head of a pin.
It is darkness,
It is pain, it is printed,
Spoken, heard, lost and found,
Ignored, silenced,
The word is . . .

The word is . . .
The word is . . .

Accept.
(Subject to revision.)

SUNDAY

Summer has arrived—for now. Thisbe and Ed are sitting on a bench at Kitsilano Beach. "How many identities do you have, Thisbe?" Ed asks. They are watching the shiny pretty people sunbathing and playing volleyball. The girls in brightly colored bikinis self-consciously pretend not to notice all the people looking, but that is why they are all there. This is what is going through Thisbe's mind, as she tries to avoid her grandmother's questions. Thisbe's learning that Ed's questions are harder to deflect than a laser beam. Her dad learned this years ago, and now it's her turn. That's Granny Ed's job: getting you to think about things you are running from and answer questions you had no intention of answering. Thisbe kicks herself, knowing that her honest nature has conspired with Ed, against her will. "Drat," she's thinking. "She did it again."

"Come on, Fiz," her granny pushes. "Are you the same person at school as you are with me? With your mom or dad? Online? With your girlfriends? I hardly think so. Which one of these versions of you would you want to meet Jason?"

That's it! Thisbe leans toward Ed. She confides in a whisper: "I want to meet him before my period started." Ed looks at Thisbe sternly and gently all at once, as if she understands her feelings but wishes they were otherwise. Thisbe sits up straight again. Her eyes water up and she blinks. A tear starts a slow journey down one cheek. Granny Ed wraps both arms firmly around her. Thisbe sobs a little more. She could have asked for the hug, but she was far too proud to do so. She probably didn't have to weep to get the hug, either, but it certainly moved things along.

She wraps both her arms around her granny and gives her a good squeeze in return.

Came home from the pool this evening (Feet Day) and went straight to the bathroom to hang up my swimming stuff. Didn't see it at first, but there was a sticky note stuck to the bathroom mirror, at about head height (i.e., about a foot above where Granny Ed's head would be). On it she'd written, like a prescription:

PLEASE REPEAT THREE TIMES A DAY (AT LEAST)
"I am a writer!"
Continue treatment until self-doubt disappears.
If symptoms continue, please consult Grandmother.
Or look in the fridge.

It certainly didn't look like Fishbone's writing. He hasn't left me a note in ages. I did look in the fridge. There was a square box in it. Inside the box was a whole, big, round, beautiful cheesecake. I hope I am ready for more cheesecake. I *don't* think I'm ready to have another big weeping fit. Granny's taken Chut for a walk. By the time she gets back, the box could well be empty.

Feet Day Report:
Thought about my feet as I swam up and down, up and down. By the end of it, I pictured myself as two feet moving side by side with a torpedo of a body attached. As if my feet

were the only part of me that was living. I watched the bubbles stream from my hands as I moved. I felt my feet in the water and wondered if fish think about how great the water feels, with warm and cold currents mingling, and how different it feels when you cross the boundaries. Cold to warm . . . Mmm . . .

Week Ten, June 4

MONDAY

What happened? Suddenly I want to write EVERYTHING ABOUT EVERYTHING. I see stories everywhere and don't know what to tune out.

Spew
Spew
Spew
I am a veritable volcano of verbiage

Overload! Texttexttexttexttext . . . . . . Addiction. Words everywhere. I'm rolling down a steep hill, and I don't know what to ignore so I gather everything like a human-sized snowball and am just waiting to crash into a tree.

So many thoughts now. So many feelings. They compete in my overcrowded brain like a track of racehorses. There is no clear winner escaping in front of the others. They arrive all at once, in a jumble of long, graceful limbs, crowding against one another. Life would be so much easier without these races. But somehow I feel as though this is the first of many.

What does this mean? How long will it last? Until I finish school? Until I leave home? Until I have written one book, two books, ten books?

RANDOM THOUGHT: How many books are inside me, waiting to get out?

I've been thinking about David, how our friendship seems invisible. I don't look at it all the time, under a microscope, like I did with Melinda and Kel. It's as if I live inside it, rather than having a friendship that's a thing, an accessory. . . . It just feels more honest. Does that make sense? When I'm around Melinda and Kel these days, I feel heavy, as if there are stones on my chest. I can't speak. It's not that I can't, really . . . It's more a feeling that I shouldn't, that I am not allowed. They've never told me to shut up. I just sense that they don't think I'm funny and clever anymore.

So what have I lost? Hope, mostly. Not a lot else, because I haven't lost a relationship, have I? There wasn't one. Or was there?? Granny E said I should tell my mom "just what happened," but I'm afraid to look stupid. Today Mom wrote she couldn't wait to get home so we can do "girl things" together. That'll be fun, I guess—as long as my dad doesn't make a big deal of it. Imagine, I can't talk to my own father about personal stuff and I just discussed it in gruesome detail with a complete stranger. A boy. Hey folks, of course you can go away and leave fourteen-year-old Thisbe on her own for twelve weeks! No problem! She'll only tell her innermost feelings to ONE boy she has never met.

Granny Ed threatened to leave Chutney here if I didn't own up to Mom. She said I would be as bad as Jason if I didn't. . . . So I guess I'll have to now. I hate being "mature."

At least she didn't blackmail me with yoga.

Made the mistake of reading publishers' Web sites. Now I am even more afraid of my career choice. I hate the idea that I will always be performing for others . . . showing off and hoping that they will like what I write. What a lot of work. So much fear.

I am seeing the world through a pinhole camera. Iphis/Jason was right about that. Sometimes I think that's all we can see. Thisbe Version 1.0 has gone. Nothing is what you think, and even if it is, you only ever see the tiniest pinprick of it. Things don't mean what you think they mean.

Inside my camera, the words I need to describe the world are crowding around the pinhole. The words are squashed, cramped, hiding in the dark.

My words have the consistency of clouds. They are shapeless, hanging in the air. They change shape; they metamorphose into things I didn't mean. I cringe. They cheat and mystify, changing color and texture and often dissolving into their particles. "Well?" they ask, as they vanish. "Whatever made you think we were yours?"

How could I have got this so wrong? Words aren't eternal at all. Not in the way I thought. You can't leave them behind and live forever. It's not that easy. These words travel through you; these thoughts visit so quickly, so quickly that they often pass by before you've had a chance to describe them.

These words—even these words I am writing, right now—may be my allies, doing my work, but they aren't my *subjects*. I am not their ruler, only their guardian. I can use them. I can borrow them. But I don't own them. They are *not* in my kingdom. . . . Perhaps I am in theirs?

My emails from Iphis/Jason look like something completely different to me now. Of course he's not into malls. And there was no makeup when he cried on me. And of course, he loved the idea of being the guy in the poem, leaving out the "spiced dainties" and secretly watching his ladylove undressing, while that rich fabric "creeps rustling to her knees." He was watching me from inside MY stories, MY assignment. My private space, my thoughts . . . Iphis thought I was the queen of foreshadowing? Looks like he's been swimming in his delicious irony since we (sort of) met. Now I know how a character in a novel would feel if she suddenly realized she wasn't real. . . . That's me. A tiny part in Jason's story. Wow. This was never Thisbe's Kingdom after all, but something quite different and much weirder.

All that time he was running the conversation. His plan, not mine. I was auditioning for a part and I didn't even know to get stage fright. I don't even know what part it was, but I think I can guess. I mean, WE VIRTUALLY SHOWERED TOGETHER. Virtually. Ha ha. Ha?

I mentioned this to Granny Ed. I thought she would be shocked. Took the whole of the walk back from the store to spit it out. Instead, she laughed. Laughed! You just can't rely on the elderly to be conservative these days. She said I should be happy with the liberties I can take online, but she'll deny saying this if I repeat it to my mom. She was practically married before she got to showering with Grandpa Michael. (Afterward it occurred to me: What is "practically married"?) I'm glad—overall—that she told me this, because I was thinking of setting up an email address for her. I can't: she'd cause havoc.

TUESDAY

I was going to make an appointment with my counselor at school today. I had planned to tell her the whole story.

Here is the whole story, then—or at least a synopsis. Let's rehearse before sharing it with my Audience. Are you paying attention? Ok, let me start. . . .

Jason knew who I was (more or less) but didn't tell me who he was (at all). His teacher knew who he was, but she didn't know the story of Iphis, so she just thought he had picked a cool username. She knew he was a boy in person, not a boy in real life and a girl online. Mr. Oliver knew about Iphis from me, but I didn't know that Iphis was really Jason. So Mr. Oliver thought of him as another girl, at Westerley. And now if Jason speaks to Ms. Patinsky and Ms. Patinsky speaks to Mr. Oliver, Mr. Oliver might not know that I am the girl in Jason's story, because there are other kids working online; so maybe Mr. Oliver wouldn't put Iphis (BOY/GIRL) and me together.

Not a great plot, is it? Definitely NOT one of my best stories. It's way better that I didn't meet with that counselor. I am going to write to Jason and fix this situation. I will. I will.

Then it occurred to me that the counselor would tell me to explain it to Mr. Oliver. And I would have to say WHY I even cared whether Iphis was a boy or not. It *mattered*. What if he weren't the excellent person he is, and he had to be punished? What if he were nasty and scary, after all? What if he were like that Anon guy/girl? OH NO, WAIT. What if he WAS that Anon person, back in the very beginning? Ugh—I can't think about it. Or about my floundering assignement . . .

So I came home and told Fishbone, but Fishbone didn't have any ideas. How can I change my assignment NOW? Mr. Oliver's into students showing leadership in their learning, but even HE would think I'm a total idiot. When I asked Granny Ed, she said if you ask for permission, you give people a chance to say no . . . and that I should do whatever I like for the assignment. Hand in whatever I feel like. I don't think those anti-rule rules are made for high school students, but maybe I will try.

WEDNESDAY

I have decided that there is no such thing as a "children's book." There are just good books and bad books, and I will read books that were written for children until I am 99. I went to the bookstore with Granny E, and she laughed her head off as usual. She didn't have a "teen age," because they hadn't invented it when she was growing up. "Now they have fifty-seven varieties of people, and they are all old enough to SPEND, SPEND, SPEND!" She said that last part much too loudly, and I had to hide in the "Young Adult" section of the store, miles away from all the cool stuffed animals I am not supposed to like anymore.

Picture this: I'm hiding in the "Young Adult" section, thinking that if I find these books interesting, that must mean I am one. Or a teenager. Or an adolescent (I hate that word. Makes me sound like a disease. Or an alien. "I am an adolescent! From the planet Adolescene! Take me to your leader!"). What am I? Is it possible to be a child, a teenager, and a young adult all at once in the same body?

I must have spent too long in my introvert world, because Granny donked me on the head with a stuffed lizard before I saw her coming. I told her she would have to buy it for me if it were damaged (see how sneaky I can be?), but sad to say, they build these animals to resist the tough love of my crazy grandmother as well as that of small children. But I did get a new label. I told Granny that she would have to refer to me as a YA from now on. She laughed and said she would always call me Pet, no matter how old I was. She seemed to think that—in spite of the past months—I am no different. I thought she was talking nonsense, but I still felt better. Maybe it was being whacked on the head with a fake lizard that did it.

I'm not going to wait and see how many ideas I have in my

lifetime. I will let myself know ahead of time. Check it out! Here's the message I'll put on the back of one of my many publications:

THISBE'S KINGDOM: A story about an extraordinary YA who overcomes the most enormous obstacles of her life, achieving her dream of becoming a second-rate novelist.

Thank you for choosing this excellent work of fiction! Your purchase has made the author very happy. If you enjoyed this, you might also like to read the following titles:

THE MASQUERADE OF IPHIS: A tragic tale of deceit and betrayal. Girl meets boy. Boy meets girl. Girl thinks boy IS a girl. They get along just fine until girl learns that boy is indeed a boy and, distraught, is forced to consume vast quantities of sweet, sticky dessert.

CHEESECAKE EATING FOR BEGINNERS: A difficult and dangerous pastime, eating cheesecake may induce feelings of profound sadness and bouts of hysterical weeping. Take an expert along on your first attempts. Allow them to eat most of the dessert, if necessary. And always, always eat cheesecake responsibly.

THE LONG-AWAITED WRITING MANUAL: And it was nearly even longer! This book will teach the aspiring writer how to procrastinate. With practice you, too, can allow television viewing, swimming, and vegetarian dinners with your grandmother to interrupt your best writing times of the day. Discipline? Whatever. That's all. Read the book. I have stuff to do.

Nothing from Jason/Iphis for over a week now. But I feel calmer . . . better. . . . I am thinking about my writing . . . which was what I was supposed to be doing in the first place. . . .

THURSDAY

I started writing in my journal—I wrote anywhere—because I wanted to believe, even at the age of nine, that my life was significant. That it was more significant than it seemed to be, to me. I wanted my ideas about the world to be a tool I could use, to carve something beautiful out of the rough stone that life hands us.

Most of the time I seem to be dropping both the tools and the raw materials on my fingers and toes. Curse my clumsiness! What was I thinking? Mainly that I was being clever, I suppose. . . . But there I go again, trying to carve out the perfect nostril when BAM! There goes the entire nose of my masterpiece. Plop! It lands in the middle of the sawdust on my studio floor. Me and my Big Mouth.

Bustory #3
Rode the #4 bus for a change. Great bustory potential. This is today's offering:

I'm sitting at the front—close to it. Second row, maybe. A

man gets on, apparently homeless. Long hair, unshaven. Unseasonably warm coat. He pays and moves along, pausing by the seats marked for the elderly and disabled and those with small children. He faces the bus full of people, which flinches as one body.

"I have an invisible disability," he declares.

A woman scurries toward the back of the bus, clutching her fabric bag to her chest. Her seat is now empty so the man sits down in it, to the sound of an angry diatribe from another passenger about "real disabilities, you know! What the hell kind of disability does he have anyways?" The entire bus stops breathing to listen.

Eventually, the man replies. "I am broken."

I thought about what he had said long after he'd made his exit (with extraordinary style, by the way; he fell to his knees in the aisle and thanked the bus driver for his ride). This man made me think. *Broken.* You can't always tell just by looking.

I smiled at Mr. Oliver in class today when he asked how the assignment was going. I said, "Fine." I am sure he could tell that my face was about to crack and fall off. I was terrified that he'd see the face I had on underneath. Every way I turn, I feel as though I did the wrong thing and no choice left to me is a good one. Sometimes there truly is no easy way out.

RANDOM THOUGHT: Have I sailed to the edge of my imagination and fallen off?

I have all sorts of ideas, still, and feel as though I am running after them with a butterfly net. Some of them fly pretty fast and others I catch right away.

Trouble is, I can't seem to pin them down all in a row—or in squares or circles or whatever the right shape is. The pieces are fine, but the whole is still in pieces. It feels like the time I was five and I had to find all of the pieces of a 500-piece jigsaw puzzle behind the couch and between the cushions. It was a good feeling to have found them all, even if I was the one who had hidden them from the babysitter the night before. I was so excited! Then my mother pointed out that having the pieces wasn't enough. We had to put the picture back together again for Nicole, whose pastoral landscape I had pulled apart in the first place. I didn't particularly dislike her. I can hardly remember what she looked like now. It's just that pulling the thing apart and hiding the pieces seemed like tons of fun at the time.

So there is my assignment, hidden in parts behind pieces of furniture, and not even twelve more weeks or help from my gran or talking to Jason will help. DAMN.

I'm still thinking about that homeless guy on the bus. I wonder if Jason is broken? I can't tell. Do I still like him as a "him"? How would I know? How could I? Doesn't being a boy mean that he is now someone new? Not to himself, of course, but to me? I wonder what he thinks about his masquerade. . . . I can't imagine being thought of as a boy.

I can't picture his face. I can picture David's face, though, and I wonder if I should tell him about Iphis/Jason. Hmm. I don't know if David is broken, but there sure are some cracks. He loves his grandpa a lot—like me. That's got to leave a crack in a person. And now his grandpa is so sick. I can see from David's face how that hurts him. Jason?? I don't really know what he's like to his mom or his sister. What was all that yelling in their house about? Maybe Jason did some of the yelling? I mean, he says he is the peacemaker but you never know.

I learned today that Granny's First Rule of Everything is that what has been said cannot be unsaid. All you can do is stop regretting your stupid mistakes and focus on how you are going to change things in the future. Then she said, "Breeeeathe . . . in through your nose and out through your mouth." At that moment I was afraid this was it—she was finally ready to drag me off to one of her granny yoga classes. SHEER TERROR FOR AN INSTANT!! But she didn't. I remain safe (for now) and need not worry about crossing my feet behind my head.

<u>Back to the plot:</u> she said that I could decide to let go of Jason, but it had to be a decision and not just running away angry. You know, I had a feeling that a speech was coming. Adults don't usually let go after one big boo hoo and the

declaration that you have learned sooooo much. Granny Ed is not to be fooled. She sees right through you.

FRIDAY

Today I asked Granny Ed what happiness is. I also asked her how you measure it. This is how our conversation went:

ME: How do you measure happiness, Granny?
GRANNY ED: By the thickness of my ankles!

Proof, once again, that my grandmother is incapable of taking anything seriously. I didn't need to get angry, because she stopped grinning and straightened up quickly. Must have been the withering look I gave her—I learned that from Mr. Oliver. I'm sure he's not really angry when he does that, but it still gets our attention.

Gran and I had a good conversation after that. She talked about eating and sleeping well, and getting enough exercise. I thought she might bring out some yoga visual aids, but she didn't. She said that if you are happy, you shouldn't know it. You should be too busy enjoying life to stop and think "Hello, Self! Self, how are you? Are you ok? 100% ok or 50%?" She said I ask myself too many questions. It's fine to relax and watch the world go by. I would ignore most of it, absorb some of it, and by the time I was 30, life would suddenly make sense.

This confused me, of course—and not just because she was

thinking about me at the age of 30. Whoa. So old. It was the idea that I shouldn't ask so many questions. I frowned. "But hey, you're the person who told me that I shouldn't stop asking questions until I am dead! You're contradicting yourself!"

She smiled. "You should never stop asking yourself questions about other people. When you figure out what shape other people are, then you will know what shape you are." She paused. "You can't know yourself by staring inward all the time. Life isn't an exam that you can fail. There's room for everyone on the planet, Fiz—just as there's room for all the books."

RANDOM THOUGHT: If there were a food chain with books in it, which books would be at the top? Which books would be vegetarians?

SATURDAY
<u>Bustory #4</u>
The old trolley bus moves along, swaying like a ship. It whines and screeches, it barks like a sea lion. It turns corners with a rattling of poles and cables that regularly disengage from one another and send the driver leaping down the stairs, pulling on a pair of gloves, to put them right. I have watched this many times, thinking that the drivers look like they're flying huge metal kites; or maybe the bus is stranded, straddling the intersection like that sea lion on a rock. Or they are at a rodeo, trying to lasso some vast, obsolete,

clanking cow. At any rate, I always end up comparing those buses to animals. . . .

This time, the bus travels without mishap. It turns onto Broadway, and as we turn, I gasp and grip the bunch of flowers in my lap. Through the bus's windshield, a vast silver shape is visible. The moon, burning a pale ghostly color, hangs heavily in the night sky.

"Wow!" I say to the bus driver, who's just a few seats away.

"Yup," says the driver, "pretty amazing."

I am glad. And I'm grateful that the bus driver has a soul, my own is hurting so much. Tonight I could break plates on the head of anyone who couldn't appreciate that moon.

The bus heaves to a halt at the stop by the bakery. A young woman climbs heavily up the stairs, visibly burdened by the backpack she carries. She drops her money in the fare box. It's an endless stream of dimes she's collected for months, years, or her whole life. I watch in disbelief, on and on it goes, until the last one makes it up to $2.00. I grit my teeth. As the bus pulls out, the woman turns around in sandaled feet, sits down, and exclaims: "Holy smokes! Just look at that moon!"

"Yup," the bus driver and I say in unison.

Suddenly I like Change Lady.

Next, the bus pauses to collect an elderly gentleman carrying a plastic bag. He climbs aboard slowly, pays his fare, and sits down on my right. He takes a deep breath and mutters to himself. What he says makes the driver chuckle and the two passengers near him smile: "That moon!"

"It's special, isn't it?" I reply, wanting to show the older man that not all teenagers are lost, lazy, or self-absorbed. I, too, can appreciate nature.

The gentleman reaches into his bag, which I now see has a picture of a parrot on it, and pulls out a long, narrow cardboard box. "This here's for you," he says simply. He extends his hand and gives me a stick of incense. I reach forward to accept the gift.

After a moment, I pull on a carnation in the bunch I am carrying for Ed and reach out. "This, here, is for you." He takes it in his surprisingly small hands and clutches the plastic bag between his thin knees. As I watch, puzzled, he breaks the stalk so that there are only a few inches left. He drops the rest of the stalk into his bag, and carefully inserts the carnation into the collar of his jacket. He has made himself a boutonniere.

"And this," he says quietly, smiling, "might change my luck this evening." He doesn't make eye contact for more than a second, but he keeps on smiling. Tonight will be an elegant occasion, and Ed won't miss one stalk.

I look out the window and think "I have no grace."

SUNDAY

I think I understand now: I wrote in my journal as a way of being not just me, Thisbe, but more than me—the über-me. Not an accurate account of me, the person, but a central character in my own "plot." The protagonist. But what is the point of being the author and the central character if you don't create the story? No point, really—you let life happen and write it down as it goes by. Like me and my bustories.

But I know why I did it. I felt like a footnote, or a margin scribble, in the story of my own life. My parents were hogging the limelight with their own publications, while I waited in the wings. Ok, so my metaphors are out of control, but there it is. The journal was a place to regroup, lick wounds, rant, be invisible, tell myself how things have been (with a little poetic license thrown in) so that I had something to believe in. But I have learned that you can't always believe what you read . . . especially if YOU wrote it in the first place.

You can't always believe what you see, feel, or hear. I didn't hear what Iphis was trying to tell me for weeks. There were so many clues. I hope he is ok.

Stupid Thisbe! You simply write as you see things, in that flawed, sudden, childish, full-of-holes kind of way. To add meaning to your boring life—but now that I am a whole two months older than I was when I started this assignment that has become everything I do, everything I am . . . well, it looks like something else. I look like something else. And my choices . . . well, they look kind of ridiculous.

News of the Bizarre: I'm beginning to love Chutney. Maybe I'm losing my mind, but he doesn't smell anymore. Is that POSSIBLE? I didn't sniff him all that closely, but it was actually possible to breathe in when he was sitting there all happy, with his tongue hanging out. Very, very mysterious.

Went swimming. Tried to do my Granny Homework. Knees Day. But I couldn't think about my knees all that much—I was too sad. Actually, swimming when you're sad is great. Nobody can see your face when you are plodding up and down. They are all too focused on themselves and their own bodies, wondering if they are sleek and silky enough in the water. I cried today, while I was swimming my lengths. My foggles weren't leaking—I was. I stopped halfway through a lap to wash them out. I was just so, so sad, I couldn't hold it together, even with Granny E's help. It felt weirdly good to be that sad on my own, though. This time I didn't want to run back and tell her so that she could make it better. I wanted to make it all better myself.

I wonder how many other people have cried into that pool this week? How much of the pool water is really other people's tears? Do we swim unknowingly through other people's tears all the time? What foolish creatures we are.

Sometimes I feel so OLD. Why?

Week Eleven, June 11

MONDAY

<u>Alone</u>
Tonight I wept on my QWERTYUIOP
I cried so hard I couldn't stop
I keep trying to write to you
But nothing comes—
It's tough when
My heart's empty
And my hands are all thumbs.

It aches inside, this feeling so bad
And I know you're a boy
But you're still the best girlfriend
I've had.

I was listening to the radio today and realized that pop songs about l-o-v-e were beginning to make sense. ARGH. What is happening to me?!

TUESDAY

From: Thisbe
To: Iphis
Subject: are you there??

Arrggghhhhh
I went online
For English 9
But nobody was there.
I'd hoped to share some thoughts
And stories
But no one seemed to care.

———

The story ends
When we were friends.
I should have held back.
At the time I knew it—
But I said more than I should.
You know it, Jason, I blew it.

Jason. Please log in. Tell me you're there. Tell me you're ok. Come back?

I spoke too soon. There I was, chuckling behind my hand, thinking I was SO CLEVER, when whammo! Granny ambushed me. Next thing I knew, we were going to a GRANNY yoga class. I don't know how she did it. She must have got special permission. And my will was possessed.

It wasn't at all what I expected. I must have been more unwilling than any student the teacher had ever had, but she was very nice. Very calm. Not at all weird, which I was mortally afraid of. She smiled at me when I came in. Probably thinking "Ah, what courage!" since I was the youngest there by at least a century. I bet she isn't used to teaching people from the Planet Adolescene.

I lay on the floor next to Gran. I stared at the ceiling tiles until I realized that we were supposed to keep our eyes shut and take deep breaths. I took the biggest breaths I could, until my head felt light and fuzzy. On the inside, that is. It's *always* fuzzy on the outside.

The teacher was very encouraging. I had to keep on peeking to work out what she wanted us to do. Sometimes I felt as though she were speaking in a code that everyone else understood. The students don't speak during the class, but it wasn't classroom not-speaking. It was happy not-speaking. I guess that means everyone was actually listening.

As I lay there curled in a ball, I started to wonder how this teacher was different from my schoolteachers. Did she have pets? Did she like her students? How could you tell? They weren't even looking at her, and she didn't mind one bit. It wasn't like a dance class. In dance, everyone's watching everyone else all the time, to see who's got a nicer outfit, who's thinner, who the teacher likes best, who's got the best shoes. In this class we were together but all alone. It was all about what was inside. Nobody looked cool. We just did our thing and didn't worry about anyone else.

Since we all had our eyes shut, I simply decided that when the teacher said "Nice!" in her lovely, warm voice, she was talking to me. But did it matter? The whole class could imagine ourselves to be her favorite. We could all go home happy. Something tells me that would make her happy, too.

I did my best, but it was very hard. I'm strong but I don't bend much, that's for sure. Still: no report card, no exam, no homework. No 84%. And you can't cheat on a yoga test by copying someone else's pose. You can't submit a pose and get it back on Thursday, covered in red ink. Nice.

WEDNESDAY

I did my Granny Ed homework again today. Swam up and down thinking of the water against my thighs. My thighs weren't used to the attention and they were a little shy at first, but they got used to it. Breathe in. Breathe out. Sigh. Thigh. Ha ha ha. By next week I might make it to my nose. . . .

Got an email from Mom. All it said was, *Still dashing about the English countryside in Lycra. Your father is simply dashing in his corduroys.* I miss them. They are with my Mom's sister now. Her name is Penelope, but my dad calls her "Catastrophe." According to her, something terrible is always about to happen. But she has an *amazing* garden, like something out of a children's story book: a rambling mess of herbs and flowers, with potatoes planted among the petunias and pansies growing out of teapots, boots, tin buckets, and chipped cups. I would love to go back there one day, to see if it really is the way I remember it.

THURSDAY

She got me again! Yoga class #2. I survived this one, also, but only just. Last time must have been beginner's luck. OUCH. The teacher was saying "breathe mindfully . . ." and I peeked. Everyone else had their eyes shut and looked as though they were breathing mindfully, but my dictionary was way over on the other side of the room, in my bag, and I couldn't exactly put my hand up and say, "Please, miss, what on Earth are you talking about?" So I shut my eyes again and pretended to be "mindful."

While we were twisted into funny shapes, the lady next to me caught my eye and smiled. I felt connected to her in some way, even though we didn't speak. But OUCH! We had to do these poses that were so hard, with our feet stretched out in the air and our heads up at the same time. My stomach was jiggling furiously with the effort, but everyone else looked calm and happy. They've no business having abdominal muscles of steel. NOT FAIR. Anyway, the teacher kindly told us that if we were in pain, we could drop any pose at any time. "Listen to your body!" she said. I listened very carefully to mine. It was saying "EEEEEOOOOOWWW! STOP!" So I crumpled onto the floor.

I don't know if I will keep going, but it was nice to go back and get used to the things the teacher said. I thought I would be bored, but it was somehow comforting. She started the class saying "Breathe deeply, let go of any disturbances . . ." and there I was, letting go of a big Melinda balloon, watching her float into space. She is definitely a disturbance in my life.

In fact, I think she is somewhat disturbed. Today she was asking me about my imaginary friend *again*. (Wow, that joke is tired). Then she turned to Kel and started laughing about how my taste in imaginary friends couldn't be any worse than my taste in REAL friends. They meant David (about whom they know NOTHING), but I immediately thought "Oh, you mean YOURSELVES! I agree." They are such small people. I started feeling angry thinking about them and how little they care about others, so I tried to take six more deep, mindful breaths to get rid of them. In the end, they just floated away, out of my thoughts. It was very nice. There goes the Melinda balloon now. . . . Bye-bye, Melinda!

Let's try a little Present-Tense Mindfulness for a description of Granny Yoga:

I'm lying on the floor, wincing, trying to keep my feet two inches off the floor and to ignore my trembling stomach. Really, I'd love to collapse like a big mound of jelly onto my yoga mat. But I won't give up. Not this time. Not when all these other people can do it.

"Relax . . . breathe . . . six more breaths now . . . don't cause any pain. You know your body," says the teacher.

"Yes," I think. "I sure do. We've just met."

The teacher walks up and down between the students. She encourages us to drop to the floor, slowly, slowly, one vertebra at a time. I do my best. Down I come, resting on the floor, moving my hands onto my stomach, breathing in and out. The teacher pauses next to me and moves my head ever so gently to one side. Behind my closed eyelids, my mind races. I expect to be annoyed, but I don't mind the teacher touching me at all.

And I wonder. How many people have actually touched me, in my life? As I breathe in and out, I count. I count my mom, my dad—although I have barely hugged him in months, oops—Granny, Grandpa Michael (those were some great hugs), my aunts and uncles in England. The list is very short. How many other people will touch me during my life? Before I can finish the thought, we are all sitting again and the class is almost over.

FRIDAY

Feeling Mindful and Present Tense-ish again. Back at school, I'm shoving more stuff into my locker. I know I should clean it, but today's not the day. Reaching into the back, I find three candy wrappers from last week and a few folded pieces of paper. I collect them up and shut my locker, sitting cross-legged on the floor to unravel the mysteries. Across the hall is another student, also cross-legged, doing her homework. I have seen this routine many times. This same girl is often at her locker, finishing homework in the minutes before school starts. It's the girl with blue hair. Not surprisingly, she doesn't look back at me.

I unfold my precious origami. The first piece of paper doesn't contain gold dust. It's a bunch of doodles. Triangles, mostly, and the name "Gwendolyne La Bon-Bon" written in fancy, curly handwriting. It's a set of scrolls and whirls, colored and blotted in leaky black ballpoint ink. Nothing interesting there. The second sheet of paper, from a lined yellow pad, yields something more intriguing. Puzzling, even. It's a poem I wrote, but I can't remember writing it. I stare at the page and read the poem twice. The poem is pretty good! I rack my brain, trying to remember when the poem came to be. I can't. I wonder, "How can you forget writing a poem? If I don't remember writing it, is it still mine?" The girl with the blue hair has finished her homework and is getting ready to pack up and sprint to class. I get up reluctantly, tucking the forgotten poem into my jeans pocket.

RANDOM THOUGHT: What if I gave up on my writing? If a novelist fails and nobody reads her work, does it make a sound?

Surprise, surprise. Melinda and her boyfriend broke up. I wasn't disgusted, outraged, staggered, or shocked, although I was stunned by the number of different words Melinda used to describe it. I was surprised it didn't make the local headlines. . . . News must have reached one or two TV stations.

I had to sit and listen to Melinda telling me that HE was an awful person, no, that SHE was an awful person—oh no, that she's "So, SO confused, I don't know WHAT to think!" (I didn't say, "Maybe the problem is that you don't know HOW to think"). Then she went on: "Maybe I should learn to be happy on my OWN and not date anyone. . . . Be more like YOU, be more independent" (sniff, sniff, sniff). She meant "a loser" like me, but like me, she was censoring herself. What a sincere, honest conversation that was. A real dialogue, a meeting of minds. I suspect Kel was hiding from her, or had been driven insane by her chatter and had her head down the toilet, flushing the lever.

In the end (and what a painful end), it all came out: Lucas thought she was "too dependent on him." This is totally shocking and devastating to Melinda. She is so used to being cool, to thinking that she is the one who has everything together. Imagine. Someone actually told HER to "get a life." He said she was "too serious." At that point, I had to stop myself from howling with laughter. . . . It has to be the first time anyone's accused her of *that*. I just sat there . . . watching poor, tormented Melinda twisting the ends of her perfectly blond hair, trying to digest the fact that she was *not* perfect, and all the time I wanted to ask, "WHY would you think I care?"

I thought of my yoga teacher and breathed in very slowly. Then I breathed out. I relaxed my face muscles, wondering if I looked any different to Melinda as I achieved this wonderful feeling of serenity in myself, but I'd have to turn into a bunch of bananas for her to notice me. Did I mention that she and Lucas have broken up? Oh. I did. Right. The "conversation" has caused me to lose some of my brain cells, which is really a shame because they were among my favorites.

I decided that Melinda's new name is Disturbance. A much better name than Melinda, and a much better name than her real one. . . . So now I am strong! Thisbe the Mighty! The Ruler of the Disturbance, who belongs to me now. The fictitious version of her, anyway, as Iphis/Jason would say. Shame I can't rename *him*, isn't it? He can't even decide on a name for himself. I wonder which name he is wearing today. Hmm. Don't think about that.

I was doing pretty well until I saw David. There we were in the cafeteria—with Disturbance yowling and howling, and Kel nowhere to be seen—when suddenly, there's David, peeking over Melinda's left shoulder. He's mouthing WHAT—ARE—YOU—DOING? and all I can do is look resigned, because if I speak to him then she will know that I'm not listening. I swear, she was so freaked out already that I think little kinks were starting to appear in her ironed hair. Eventually, David realized that I was but a small rock, caught in the massive gravitational pull that is Melinda's personality, so he started goofing around, pulling faces, and tickling his own armpits. He doesn't care what people think of him, so he feels no pressure to be "cool." Today he really outdid himself. And I really had no idea his elbows bent backward like that. Wow, Granny Ed should take HIM to yoga. Eventually, he got bored of his monkey act and went into orbit somewhere else, but not before he'd written a BIG sign on a sheet of paper, which he held up to his shirt (one finger over each nipple—nice touch, David). The sign said "SUCKER!!!!!! I'll be in the LAB."

I really hope this "horrible, horrible" experience is good for Melinda. Maybe she'll learn to be her own person now, instead of gagging and drooling over someone else. Maybe she will realize how I felt this year when she started behaving like an android. Or at least, she might start wearing jeans that come up past her butt.

RANDOM THOUGHT on why I love reading so much: it's a wonderful, rich, socially acceptable way to have imaginary friends.

Afterward, David and I were working away in the computer lab. Somehow, I managed to persuade Melinda to look for Kel so that I could escape and finish my assignment in saner company. I slumped in my chair, next to David. He'd taken his usual chair: back row, middle.

"I can't believe we weren't friends before," I told him. I was looking frazzled. My hair was disheveled where I was pulling at it in sympathy with Melinda.

"How could we have been?" asked David.

"What do you mean?"

"Er . . . to be friends, you'd have to notice that I exist." David stopped typing and looked at me.

"Was that a poke in the nose? Ow?"

"Sort of. But I don't mean to be mean. I'm not a GIRL, ha ha. I just wasn't on your radar screen," he explained.

"Right, so I couldn't shoot you down."

"Ha. You're clever. But seriously. You had major reinforcements. Those girls are like an army. The Melinda Militia. People are actually scared of them."

"If they are, they're stupid," I told him. "The only thing

you should be scared of is being dazzled by *their* stupidity. You could start talking to them as a perfectly smart person and before you know it, you'd be talking about reality TV shows. No lie. It happened to me. More than once."

"Whoa. Scary. I never will figure out how you became friends with them."

"Sorry. I was pretty careless when I was seven. And Melinda hadn't gone to the dark side then. It was more about sharing a ride to ballet and making cookies, you know?"

"I know what you mean. But I never got into the ballet thing myself," said David, smiling.

"Pity," I said. "You might have liked it. You never know until you try."

"I do know. Trust me."

"Ha ha. People do change though, don't they? I'm not talking about you getting into ballet. I'm talking about me not being friends with Melinda."

"Yep, they do. Including you. Which works well for me, I have to say."

SATURDAY

Stood on my head with the grannies again today. Somewhere in the middle of all those poses and rests and shifting and rocking from side to side, I noticed that there were two voices in my head. Not "VOICES" that people worry about. Both of them were my thoughts. But I was listening and watching them appear in my head. I was putting on a show. Then the Audience version of me, sitting in a comfy chair and watching the thoughts go by, would say: "Ah, that was profound!" "Oh no, you are getting yourself all confused . . ." "No no no . . . forget about that altogether."

We did the Fish Pose today. The teacher said it was a very loving, open pose. I had NO idea what she was talking about. I was too busy thinking how odd it was to have two streams of thought going at the same time. Suddenly it came to me that I had all this LOVE. I would never, ever, EVER mention this to Melinda and Kel, but while I was lying there—my hands clenched under my butt, with my head tipped back at this impossible angle—I thought that I could almost hug those nasty girls. It wouldn't cost me anything, and they'd sure be surprised. Really, I didn't care what they thought of me. . . . All I could think about was doing the Fish Pose every day before school so that I could be filled with lurve for my fellow students.

And then it got even wackier. I pictured myself in the Fish Pose on one of Anna-Lisa's stamps. She's gone back to fish, having given up on reptiles: there simply weren't enough snake and lizard stamps to make a difference to her collection. There she is, sorting stamps at a small desk by an open window. She looks up to see the Cowboy Oliver tipping his hat at the sheriff. She goes back to her collection, gazing with great affection at the stamp with me on it. I'm one of her favorites. Into her book I go.

Wow. I'm DEFINITELY not going to mention this to David. Right now, I think my stock is pretty high. This would really make him look at me with that expression that says, "I'll be patient and speak very slowly, because this Earthling is missing some vital genes, which makes her more than a little foolish and subject to strange imaginings. Keep under observation for further understanding of the species. . . ."

Wish I could tell Jason.

BREAKING NEWS: Lucas and Melinda never had sex. I don't think she even saw the Paragon of His Masculinity. Ha ha ha ha . . . I wonder which one of them didn't want to. I was so sure that Melinda did. Maybe she didn't? Maybe *he* didn't? Maybe he did some soul-searching (between cigarettes) and discovered that he is deeply conservative? Whatever. Just shows you can't judge a gal by the low rise of her jeans.

SUNDAY

Went swimming with Gran again today. Or rather, floating. As we floated, we talked about my homework: how I was supposed to be thinking about the different parts of my body. Had to confess that I'd only got up to my thighs so far. Granny Ed said it didn't matter. She said we could do laps until I'd made it to my nose. So we did. I did twice as many laps as she did, but we finished together. Every time I passed her, she waved and asked me where I had got to. If anyone else was listening, it would have sounded like this:

> Conversation #1
> [Sound of splashing]

Granny Ed: Well?
Me: Bottom

Conversation #2
[Sound of splashing]
Granny Ed: Well?
Me: Waist

And so on. Anyway, I finished my homework, but I sense that the assignment is something I'm supposed to do every week. We'll see how that goes. Unlike the stuff at school, Granny Ed's assignment really does feel *Authentic.*

Still no news from Iphis-Jason. Will he ever contact me again? What will I do with our assignment? Granny Ed has been nagging me to figure this out. She says that I shouldn't wait until he writes to me to think it through. I should figure it out in advance and know where I stand, without expecting someone else to help me get there.

Argh. I think I actually need to do a "reflection" (GASP).

<u>What Thisbe Learned This Spring</u>
I learned that killing mosquitoes is about the wrist action and the tomato sauce, not about the choice of weapon. I learned that when you are 70, it is perfectly acceptable to swim in your underwear and NOBODY cares. I learned that wordplay is amusing (or do I mean "punny"?). I learned that yoga is not just about knowing how to stand on your head. And that you definitely shouldn't judge a book by its

cover. Some books, like the people who read them, aren't what they seem to be. . . .

RANDOM THOUGHT: If my life were a book, what would be on the cover? Would people judge me by it? Should they?

Later that same day . . . No, no, no. I don't need another reflection. . . . I need a page of acknowledgments.

I would like to thank the following people for helping me achieve my tremendous fame and success:

My mom and dad, Annabel and Timothy, for buying me a computer. Without it, I would ALWAYS have to write by hand and would never be published during my lifetime. Also, for being great readers themselves and for loving words so much.

Melinda and Kel, for helping me to become a social outcast. This gave me time to write.

David, for showing me that I WASN'T a social outcast, so I would actually feel like writing.

Granny Ed, for filling my tummy with veggies, so I didn't pass out from hunger while writing. For swimming in her undies, and giving me something to write about. For bringing the dishwasher back to life, and giving me something to write about. For the sticky note on my mirror. Ditto for whacking mosquitoes with spaghetti sauce, inventing Knees Day, and (although I haven't said this to Gran yet) for taking me to yoga so I wouldn't be too tense and freaked out to write. But mostly, for learning to feed Chutney raw dog food instead of that nasty canned stuff. Smelly dog no longer smells!

Jason, for listening to me. For reading my words. For being serious.

For being silly. For drawing pictures of me with GREAT hair!

My companion. My muse. My yogi . . . Fishbone. From whom I learned everything I know about "stillness" and "breathing mindfully." I have not learned to purr yet, but trust that with Fishbone's excellent instruction, this is not far off.

And finally: Grandpa Michael, who still manages to wink at me, through Granny Ed.

To all of you, I am deeply grateful.

Ah, my parents, returning this week from the Land of Eng: my tall, graceful mother, who should have been called Guinevere . . . except that she married the court jester instead of the king. My mother is still beautiful. She has long, slender fingers. The prettiest hands I have ever seen. Unlike mine, which are small and square and have little sausage fingers. My mother is very precise. My father is a scattered artist with big feet. Sort of like me, I suppose—apart from the feet. I never thought of that before. Gran and I have both been in something of a panic, cleaning the house in time for their return. My mom keeps everything so tidy. Gran worked VERY hard on the kitchen. Is she a little afraid of my mom?

I think I might miss getting emails from my dad, although a lot of his messages lately have been about bathrooms that haven't been renovated since 1850.

RANDOM THOUGHT: David's grandfather has nightmares, but when he wakes up, he can't open his eyes and chase away the awful pictures with the real world. He can open his eyes, but he still sees the same thing as if they were closed.

I think there's a poem in this . . . and I don't feel like making any bad jokes about his blindness or his visions.

David's Grandfather Has Nightmares
Bad dreams
Shake him awake.
There's no rest
No shift
No break.
Eyes open but
There is no light:
There is no comfort
In the night.

You know, I am beginning to wonder if I'm a little selfish. I don't just listen to David's stories about his grandpa because I like him and I want them both to be ok—although I do, and I do. Part of me wonders if I am listening because I miss Grandpa Michael and I envy David. He still gets to spend time with his grandfather.

I read my poem to Granny Ed. And then I told her about being selfish. She looked at me with a completely straight face and an expression I couldn't name. All she said was, "I miss him, too. Sometimes I can't sleep, either."

Week Twelve, June 18

MONDAY

I did a bad thing today. I couldn't help myself. I was stuffing books into my locker when the bell rang and everyone started the stampede back to class. I was last (what a surprise) and as the hall cleared, I noticed a piece of paper on the floor. It had fallen out of someone's locker and was just lying there, practically begging me to read what was on it.

So I did. And it was a poem. It was a really, really good poem. And the worst part of all this—worse even than me reading someone's stuff in secret—is that it's by someone who has every right to hate me. . . . It's by the girl with blue hair. Her name is Ally. I didn't know that before, but I do now. And I wish I could tell her how much I liked her poem. Here it is:

> Not Home in My Skin
> There's nobody here so
> Please leave a message
> Speak clearly at the tone
> I don't give my address
> Over the phone
> I'm not really here
> This is just a visit
> Even though this *is* life—or is it?

As usual, I talked to Granny Ed. She said it wasn't fair of me to expect a friendship with this person just because I've discovered she's a writer. She said that would be "self-serving." I tried to explain that I already felt bad about making those jokes. I never disliked her. I don't even know her. Gran suggested that I find a way to return the poem and that if I wanted to, I might let her know that I had found it, read it, loved it, and had given it back without telling anyone else at school. She said I should sign my note, and maybe give her some of my own writing, "as a peace offering."

What will I say? What a difficult note.

TUESDAY

From: Jason
To: Thisbe
Subject: *approaches cautiously*

Thisbe, it's me, Jason. New ID, same person as before, different person from the one you imagined. This is the Jason who apologizes, the Jason who misses you, who's been around the world and back, scouring the Amazonian rain forests for your boots as a memento.

I had to write. Something happened, and I can't tell my mom or Sienna and I can't tell the guys at basketball. Well, you know, I need to talk to you. What do you say?

Granny Ed hears Thisbe let out a yelp upstairs. She puts down the pot she is wiping and walks toward the stairs. She's shuffling a little because she's wearing an old pair of Timothy's slippers. They are enormous on her small feet, but she's been wearing them because they make her feel at home. She grasps the bottom of the banister and climbs.

She pushes gently on Thisbe's bedroom door with one hand and knocks with the other. She peeks in to see Thisbe turned around in her chair, mid-gasp. Her hands are still over her mouth, and it takes her a second to speak.

"He came back, Gran! What do I do?"

Ed approaches and sits down on the bed next to Fishbone. "You write back, of course. But do it calmly. Don't rush. Think about what you want to say. He wrote you an email, I suppose?"

"Yes," replies Thisbe.

"Well, then. Just hang on. Write in your journal about something completely different. Don't hurry back to him, as flustered as you are. First, forgive yourself. Then you can worry about forgiving him. Ok?" Ed waits a moment.

Thisbe nods, looking very uncertain. "I think so, Gran. I can do that."

"You will, pet. I'll go back to cleaning up. When you're ready, we can go for another walk. It's beautiful outside. That'll do us both good. All right?"

"All right."

"Good. You'll be fine, dear. See you in a bit." Granny Ed gets up, strokes the top of Fishbone's head, kisses Thisbe on the forehead, and leaves. She closes the door behind her and goes back downstairs, shuffling all the way in Timothy's enormous slippers.

266

When she enters the kitchen, Timothy and Annabel look up from the piles of mail they are sorting. They returned this morning, at last, and are extremely jet-lagged. Annabel asks how Thisbe is doing. Granny Ed smiles a serene smile and says, "Oh, she's just fine."

I don't really care anymore whether I have an Audience or not. It used to be the most important thing. I wanted people to read what I wrote and that was the huge thing for me ... but now I would do it whether or not anyone was reading it. So I may as well get on and do it alone. I don't need to wait for the music to come on, so that I can dance for other people.

I am going to dance to the music in my head, and I don't care who sees me.

Breathe, Thisbe. Breathe. Mindfully. In. Out. These words are not mine. They are only passing through me. Words will come. Let them come. Words will go. Let them go.

I talked to Mr. Oliver after class today. I actually smiled at him and told him my project was going ok. I guess I found the glue to repair the pieces of my Humpty Dumpty face, to put myself together again, because he smiled back and said he was happy to hear it. Then he said, "Don't worry if it feels too difficult. Sometimes you might think your writing is terrible ... but don't give up! It'll come together."

I bet Mr. Oliver has written an unpublished novel. I wonder

if he'd ever let me see it. He's seen enough of *my* writing by now.

QUICK! Be random! Don't think about Jason!

Ok. Let's see: I went into the cafeteria at lunch. They had "jalapeño corn dogs" on the menu. It sounded like the title. of an email spam. Went off to the lab to eat leftovers instead. (Message to Norm: may a thousand little angels throw rose petals in your path, for teaching Granny Ed to make those flat noodles.)

I took the plunge and returned Ally's poem with a note. I told her how great I thought her poem was. Shoved my parcel through the slots in her locker door. Followed Gran's advice and included some of my writing, too. SCARY. She's the only person I've ever shared my writing with at school. I'm smart, eh? Starting with someone who doesn't even like me. Hope that makes me the "mature" and "selfless" person I pretended to be when my parents left for England. . . .

Breathe mindfully. Bring your knees to your chest, grasp your knees with both hands, and rock from side to side.

All those crazy yoga poses. In one class, I can be a Down Dog, an Angry Cat, a Tree, a Mountain, a Warrior, a Child, a Chair, an Open Window, a Cobra, a Fish, a Butterfly, and a Sphinx. Maybe it's not that weird to be a Child, a Young Adult, and a Woman in the same body.

Oh—and my parents are back. At least their bodies are. I think their minds are on a later flight. Their enormous mound of luggage arrived ok, though. Still waiting to see how much of it is "material" for their books, and if there's anything for me in there.... It feels as though they were gone for a year. They set off when I was still friends with Melinda and Kel, more or less. Well, *less*. When we were leaving school today, Melinda said good-bye at the lockers. She had an odd look on her face, and it took me a second to realize what the look was. It was the old Melinda, as if she had come back, but only for a split second. I thought she was going to say something about how things used to be with us, but if she was, she changed her mind. She shut her locker door, said "See ya," flicked her hair out of her hoodie, and off she went. Bye-bye, Disturbance.

From: Thisbe
To: Jason
Subject: Re: *approaches cautiously*
I say yesohmygod, Jason of the Golden Fleece! I'm so relieved. I missed you so much. I was sure you'd gone for good. I won't blab this time (be quiet, Fiz!). What happened? I AM SO SORRY. *thinks "Rats . . . I promised Gran I'd be calm"*

Stay CALM, Thisbe. Distract yourself! Write something completely different here. How about a commercial for Norm's Noodles? Ok, let's see . . .

*Is your life empty? Is your tummy crying out
for something new? Weep no more!*
jingle starts*
*EAT NOODLES! Eat oodles of Norm's Nummy Noodles!
What a meal! You'll never forget it. You won't regret it.
EAT NORM'S NUMMY NOODLES NOW!*

From: Jason
To: Thisbe
Subject: a proper apology

First, I want to say I'm so sorry about everything. I took a good beating (Sienna walks softly but carries a big stick) . . . and realized that honesty isn't only the best policy, it is the ONLY policy. I shouldn't have let you go on believing the untruth. I should have told you. . . . If I have to humiliate myself and say sorry every day of our friendship, I will. I will never lie to you again. I promise. Our friendship is more important to me than anything right now. Those hugs were real. I will never, ever let you down again.

From: Thisbe
To: Jason
Subject: a proper apology?

Please . . . get up . . . I can't bear to see you on your knees like that. Come on, GET UP. The hugs were real from me, too. I'm prepared to have another one, but I might be a bit shy about it. I was so afraid that you would think I was a flirt.

From: Jason
To: Thisbe

Subject: really, a proper apology

There's nothing wrong with flirting . . . but I understand that this isn't that kind of hug. This is the kind that leaves soggy patches on Fiz's shoulder again.

From: Thisbe
To: Jason
Subject: soggy

Tell me you're wearing mascara this time?

From: Jason
To: Thisbe
Subject: whatever you like

I'll wear a dress if you want me to.

From: Thisbe
To: Jason
Subject: get help here

C'mere and snuggle. Tell all. Fishy and Fiz are here to listen. Fishy's all ears and so am I.

From: Jason
To: Thisbe
Subject: Re: get help here

So here it is (nice cuddly shoulder, by the way): I was wandering home from the record store. I see some people sitting at the window in an Indian restaurant. They are totally locked on each other. Focused. Holding hands, doing the whole gaze intently, I-only-have-eyes-for-you thing.

I don't think anything of it. People get mooshy, even in middle age, right? Right. So I'm just looking at nothing when suddenly I see that *it's my dad*, and there he is with his new whatever she is, and they don't see me (I know, he never REALLY saw me—ever—that's why I am so angry). . . . And all I can think is "What are you doing? You are supposed to be in OREGON!"

I'm so angry I can hardly breathe, but I also feel as if I'm going to throw up right there, so I keep on walking and the next thing I know I'm pushing the button at the crosswalk and on I go, on I go, on I go . . . until I get home. And I know it's home, but it feels as though someone has huffed and puffed and the house has blown down. . . . I just can't see the rubble yet.

From: Thisbe
To: Jason
Subject: Re: Re: get help here
Ah. Ah. Ah. Ow. My brain is racing. My brain is doing squirlies on the surface like a silver bug on a lake. Give me a minute to read what you wrote again?

Your house is still standing, Jason. Your mom is there. Sienna is there. I am there. Your dad is not there, but you DON'T need him for your house to be standing. It's as strong as it always was. We are all in it. Are you listening to me?

From: Jason
To: Thisbe
Subject: I'll huff and I'll puff and I'll blow the house down. . . .
Of course, of course. I know—and thank you. But it's still sinking

in. I mean, I knew but I didn't really know. I still feel sick. And yes, the house is still standing, but it's not quite the same as the house I used to know. . . .

From: Thisbe
To: Jason
Subject: no, not homeless
But it will keep you safe. We will keep you safe. You are not homeless, friend.

From: Jason
To: Thisbe
Subject:

. . . .

From: Thisbe
To: Jason
Subject: Re:
Talk to me. What did you do when you got home? Did you take deep breaths and drop shoulders? Did you drink tea? Did you listen to soothing music?

From: Jason
To: Thisbe
Subject: Re: Re:
None of these. Got angry. Walked until my feet hurt. Switched computer on. Wrote to you.

From: Thisbe
To: Jason

Subject: Re: Re: Re:
Dangerous. Emailing when angry is like driving under the influence. Trust me. I found out the hard way. . . . Are you sure it's safe? *gives Jason's hand a reassuring squeeze—the right kind of squeeze*

From: Jason
To: Thisbe
Subject: I'm ok . . . really
I think I'm safe now. The walls of my house are moving back to where they should be. Everything is in slow motion. Alone at home, and mom at work. Memory comes back. . . . My stomach turns over every time I think of his gooey expression, seeing them touch. *pauses to breathe*
I should go to the beach, probably. Chill. Take it easy.

From: Thisbe
To: Jason
Subject: don't believe you, sorry
I can tell from here that you aren't breathing properly. Man, I'm going to take you out and subject you to some extreme yoga. Breeeeeaaathe. . . . In and out through your nose. Count to four as you breathe out. Are you doing it? Be honest.

From: Jason
To: Thisbe
Subject: Re: don't believe you, sorry
Ok, I'm doing it now. Your grandmother finally got you to go to yoga?! Anyway, I think it's helping. But I'm still angry. I feel as though I've been punched and my hands are tied behind my back.

I want to punch him, too, but I can't move.

From: Thisbe
To: Jason
Subject: poor you
Poor Jason, the peacemaker, wanting to punch someone. Maybe you do need that counselor after all . . . to "share". . . . This is not good . . . but YOU KNOW I am right there with you, even if I am not literally right there with you?

From: Jason
To: Thisbe
Subject: poor me
. . . I know. . . . But if you don't mind . . . I will stick with the fantasy that you are holding me up for now. . . .

From: Thisbe
To: Jason
Subject: poor you
Go ahead. I have been a bad friend. I will learn, I promise . . . but . . . can I change the subject . . . is that ok? Can we talk about something else, too?

From: Jason
To: Thisbe
Subject: Re: poor you
Ssss . . . . . . *sound of exhalation . . . followed by a hiccup . . .* You probably should.

From: Thisbe
To: Jason
Subject: could we . . . ?
approaches gently to the sound of cracking eggshells Could we talk about the assignment? We have only two days left and my work is a MESS. I have bits and pieces everywhere. I need your help. *chews nervously on hangnail; spits it out*

From: Jason
To: Thisbe
Subject: Re: could we . . . ?
Sure. Mine is—well—not there. Eleventh hour, last minute. Was planning to stay up all night tomorrow and write down whatever came to mind. Ms. Patinsky loves twentieth-century novelists. She'll think it's "stream of consciousness" and give me an A+, ha ha ha ha. Ha?

From: Thisbe
To: Jason
Subject: Re: Re: could we . . . ?
I wouldn't be so sure. In the event that the cabin loses pressure and you are forced to reach for oxygen . . . what are your other emergency exits for this assignment?

From: Jason
To: Thisbe
Subject: assignment SOS
Well . . . I've really enjoyed being your Audience. I'm happy to say so. I can write about your writing, about your writing process with me involved, about my identity as a reader, as a

member of "your" audience. . . .

From: Thisbe
To: Jason
Subject: Re: assignment SOS
Stream of consciousness, there you go . . . nice . . . ☺ *smiles reassuringly* They all sound like good ideas, especially the last one. Since your identity isn't the one I had imagined, I had thought of writing about the topic "Can you ever really know your Audience?" What do you think of that?

From: Jason
To: Thisbe
Subject: knowing your audience
I think I'm NERVOUS. Are you going to write about my unmasking? Please don't. My heart's pounding as it is. . . .

From: Thisbe
To: Jason
Subject: Re: knowing your audience
You're right. I don't want the Oliver-Patinsky army to arrest you! Let's finish our assignments, keep it academic and "collaborative" or whatever, get a stupid grade, get on with being friends . . . or . . . ? We might even meet one day. I do want to meet you, if you want to and if my parents say ok. Hey, I want THEM to meet you. I hope they won't worry. Should I? Is this one of those Fourteen-Year-Old-Really-Poor-Judgment Moments? Am I not being "mature"?

From: Jason
To: Thisbe
Subject: Re: Re: knowing your audience
Your parents absolutely should worry. We might like each other in person. We might hold hands. It could get messy.

From: Thisbe
To: Jason
Subject: er . . . ?
MESSY? Were you planning to shove your hand in the peanut butter jar before you reached for mine? Now, that's more romantic than being sold for a coupla camels. Smooth or chunky, then?

From: Jason
To: Thisbe
Subject: Re: er . . . ?
Smooth. But that's me, not the peanut butter, ha ha ha. I was thinking more along the lines of whipped cream. I'll get you yet. Squish.

From: Thisbe
To: Jason
Subject: *dodges flying dollop of cream*
Just hold your horses (and that whipped cream) for a sec, ok? I have an offering for you . . . food for thought, kinda. I've been typing in another document during our chat; that's why I've been a bit slooooow. Are you ready to read?

From: Jason
To: Thisbe
Subject: ok
Er . . . yeah?

From: Thisbe
To: Jason
Subject: Re: ok
And by the way? I am throwing away my mom's "natural" peanut butter. I think it has turned into a Newtonian liquid. Is that possible?

From: Jason
To: Thisbe
Subject: not ok
No, it's not! SHOWTIME!

From: Thisbe
To: Jason
Subject: finished poem, perhaps
Here it is . . .

> Leavings
> Love is not like glue.
> It cannot stick people together
> Because you want it to.
> You might think this is all,
> This is my world and what there is—
> But nothing is forever.
> I might love you and you might
> Love me, but we are unglued, unstuck.
> We have no time, you've gone
> With her. I'm out of luck. I miss
> Our nights in, the conversations
> We had—I know I'll forgive you
> One day, but not yet, Dad.

From: Thisbe
To: Jason
Subject: Re: finished poem, perhaps
Well? You aren't saying anything. Am shaking here. Are you still there? Are you upset?

From: Jason
To: Thisbe
Subject: wow
Choked up. My sister will love you. You must come to my house and have dinner. No spiced dainties, promise.

From: Thisbe
To: Jason
Subject: *says nothing; looks at feet and blushes*

From: Jason
To: Thisbe
Subject: Re: *says nothing; looks at feet and blushes*
The world doesn't end at your keyboard. There is no sign saying "Here Be Dragons."

From: Thisbe
To: Jason
Subject: er . . .
Feels somewhat nervous; wonders if she is supposed to exercise caution and be unusually mature. It feels ok

From: Jason
To: Thisbe

Subject: in the swim

Oh, wait! I nearly forgot. Here's you: the new version of you . . . in your element.

Thisbe, swimming in her words.

From: Thisbe
To: Jason
Subject: Re: in the swim
Gosh. It really is me. I love it. I mean "me." Er. You know what I mean. . . . *bats at a few stray words*

From: Jason
To: Thisbe
Subject: Re: Re: in the swim
Can you accept it from me? I hope it's not too soon.

From: Thisbe
To: Jason
Subject: Warning! Bad pun approaching!
Should I beware of "Geeks bearing gifts"?

From: Jason
To: Thisbe
Subject: *staggers under weight of bad pun*
Ha ha ha—you've been reading Greek mythology, I take it? Or do I mean "geek" mythology?

From: Thisbe
To: Jason
Subject: *helps Jason out from underneath pun*
Oh, trust me, I've been reading. And no, it's not too soon. I love it. Although I have started to wonder if words are ever really mine . . . if you know what I mean. This isn't really Thisbe's Kingdom we're in, after all. It's something much *stranger* than that. . . . *looks thoughtful*

From: Jason
To: Thisbe
Subject: passing notes
*Looks at Thisbe kindly, gently reaches across library table and passes a note, carefully folded in two.
   The note reads: *You Are Special**

From: Thisbe
To: Jason
Subject: well, these words are mine—and they are for you

Unfolds note gingerly, as if it will explode, reads quietly, then takes longer than you would think to read three words. Thinks: could this be Thisbe's first real love story?

From: Jason
To: Thisbe
Subject: truth or fiction
This-be no love story. Thisbe real . . . Thisbe all there is . . .
Waits patiently and respectfully; knows Thisbe will do whatever she wants, is prepared to log off and wait in the other world. Jason reaches for the string to turn off the dim lamp on his side of the library table

From: Thisbe
To: Jason
Subject: Re: truth or fiction
Thisbe quickly reaches across the table and takes hold of Jason's hand. He cannot turn off his light just yet. He must give her a minute. She slides another note back across the table.

When we have turned in our assignments, we can meet online again as our real selves, not our assignment selves. We can be friends and my parents (jet-lagged but present!) will know about you, too. Then we can pretend to be all "mature" about this. What do you say?

From: Jason
To: Thisbe
Subject: Re: Re: truth or fiction
I say: We will meet in person, then?

From: Thisbe
To: Jason
Subject: meeting
Maybe. But now I must keep my promise and go for a walk with Gran and Chutney. They are here only for another few days.

From: Jason
To: Thisbe
Subject: Re: meeting
*Jason reaches forward and switches off the lamp on his side of the table. He pauses for a moment to look at Thisbe, admiring the mess of brown curls and the way she holds her pen, delicately but with determination. He finds her graceful like her prose, quirky like her adjectives, and sharp like lemons.

He knows that she will smile if he smiles first, but he respects her writing privacy and quietly gathers his books up, slides them into one pile, and drops them into his bag. He exits the library, treading softly, nodding at the gothic librarian as he goes. He notices that the librarian is not wearing his usual pointy boots, but a pair of comfortable sandals. Something in his life has changed, too. The heavy library door swings shut. Swooosh! Iphis walks home slowly but with purpose. All this time, Thisbe is at the library table, working away . . .*

From: Thisbe
To: Jason
Subject: the calm after the storm
*Thisbe has watched Jason leave. She is sad but also excited to know that she will see the real him online in two days. She is concentrating on her work. She'll make the deadline. Granny Ed

is waiting for her downstairs. Fishbone is sleeping, kindly keeping her parents company. She's staring at Jason's last words, knowing that he will return now only as Jason. She can't wait. What is this feeling? She has company on her strange mission. She, too, reaches forward and turns off her light. She gathers up her notebook and heads for the door, noticing as she goes that the librarian is not reading Shelley or Byron this time, but a romance with shiny gold lettering on the cover*

<u>News of the Weird:</u> When my parents woke up, I brought them up to date on the goings-on at school (or rather, I gave them the heavily edited, beautifully packaged, somewhat true version). Told my dad about Mr. Oliver's facial hair, which grew to impressive proportions during their trip. When my dad stopped snorting with laughter, he told me a secret he'd learned at the last Parent-Teacher conference. Mr. Oliver HAS written a novel. He told my dad he'd sworn to grow his beard until he sells his book. Seriously. By the time he gets his name in print, we could be stepping over that beard to get to class. Mr. Oliver, Mr. Oliver, let down your beard. . . .

From: Thisbe
To: Jason
Subject: to work!!
All right: I'm back from my walk and ready to do business this time! No gooshy stuff! I've read over our emails . . . many times . . . and am wondering which bits will fit with the assignment.

From: Jason
To: Thisbe
Subject: Re: to work!!
Can we use the space scene? That was one of my favorites. The antigravity capsule was a real hoot.

From: Thisbe
To: Jason
Subject: Re: Re: to work!!
I will need to edit the part about our trip to planet Znooch. . . . The shower scene HAS to go. We could definitely use "The Tragedy of Elijah Sprout."

From: Jason
To: Thisbe
Subject: sprouting
Yes! The rest I leave to you, mademoiselle.

From: Thisbe
To: Jason
Subject: Re: sprouting
That is very generous of you, I think! What would you like to contribute to this fine piece of collaborative learning, my friend?

From: Jason
To: Thisbe
Subject: Re: Re: sprouting
Well . . . I thought up a title. I also thought I could do some artwork for the cover. And you can use my emails in your bit. Then, I could wrap up with an author biography and a short interview with you.

How you grew into the startling talent you are today, etc.

From: Thisbe
To: Jason
Subject: biography
It all sounds great, but . . . biography? What are you going to put in it?

From: Jason
To: Thisbe
Subject: Re: biography
I thought I would throw myself into the spirit of things and make up the whole thing.

From: Thisbe
To: Jason
Subject: what's in a name?
Ha ha ha ha. Sounds great. But wait . . . What are we going to call this masterpiece?

From: Jason
To: Thisbe
Subject: Re: what's in a name?
. . . .
pauses for dramatic effect
. . . .

From: Thisbe
To: Jason
Subject: Re: Re: what's in a name?
I'm waiting!

WEDNESDAY

It is the day before our assignments are due, and we are in "workshop" mode. The class works in groups, discussing the final projects. Mr. Oliver walks quietly up and down the rows, his arms folded across his chest. Today it's so hot that he's in his shirtsleeves. Melinda and Kel are looking excited. There's no way they're talking about the project.

David and I are both almost done. I told him about my stories and showed him some bits and pieces. He said I was brave, but he knows less than half of the REAL story. I didn't tell him too much about Granny Ed, and I feel a bit guilty about that. She helped me a lot.

I listened to David's account of reading to his grandfather. I'm sure he didn't tell me everything . . . but like my project, I think his isn't really finished. Or rather, the deadline may have arrived, but our Audiences won't be leaving. They are sticking around well beyond tomorrow for another show—many years, if we're lucky. I told David about how we lost Grandpa Michael. He listened very carefully. I think he realizes that being lucky isn't just about having a math brain, or being the right kind of geek.

For once, I came prepared for today's class, both for Mr. Oliver and for David. After a late dinner last night, I was mulling over the last few weeks and how I had got to know David . . . when Granny Ed suggested that I do something for him. Something in the region of a boutonniere or a stick of incense. A gift to recognize kindness, not a romantic gesture, of course (I think that last part was for my mom's benefit, who was giving me a funny look. I've been getting a lot of those since they returned). "Of course," I repeated.

David shoves the gift into his backpack almost as soon as Thisbe puts it in his hands. He barely says thank you but hopes she doesn't take this the wrong way. David's not loud when it comes to saying thank you—but he's definitely grateful. David doesn't know it, but last night, Thisbe and her granny went to the twenty-four hour drugstore and bought him this package of cassettes. Still, he knew what the tapes were for even without reading the note Thisbe had stuck to the package. Now he can read to his grandpa and record every word, so that his grandpa can hear his voice during the night, when he can't sleep. Thisbe doesn't know it, but the first story on those tapes is going to be about the quiet new friend he has made in math class. She is a bit strange, but she really has an amazing talent for writing. David thinks he's lucky. He thinks he might do all right in English this year.

From: Thisbe
To: Jason
Subject: using the dictionary
I finally looked up the spelling of Chutney's dog breed. It's D-A-C-H-S-H-U-N-D. I knew it was something without enough vowels in it. . . .

From: Jason
To: Thisbe
Subject: Re: using the dictionary
A dachshund? Are you KIDDING?! All this time you had me thinking that he was one of those big, bouncing, sloppy dogs . . . and he was just a tiny little sausage. Man, you really like to exaggerate, don't you?

From: Thisbe
To: Jason
Subject: *assumes regal pose*
Chutt-the-mutt:

I do not exaggerate, if you please. **I Am A Writer**. Ten years from now, I shall make my living through the ancient and greatly respected craft of Making Stuff Up. Consider yourself warned.

From: Jason
To: Thisbe
Subject: *gulps hard*
All right, milady. I'll bear that in mind. And now, perhaps, I should go back and read over our correspondence . . . very, <u>VERY</u> carefully. . . .

From: Thisbe
To: Jason
Subject: *winks*
Oh, quite probably. I guess you still think I have friends called Melinda and Kel.

Think again.

From: Jason
To: Thisbe
Subject: I'm thinking
Wow.

Here's what I have so far:

<u>About the Author</u>
Thisbe shows tremendous promise as an author. Her excellent vocabulary and firm grasp of irony are remarkable, especially for a teenager, and will be sure to attract a loyal following. Her granny,

Ed, helped bring warmth and a sense of humor to her work. Thisbe's cat, Fishbone, also had a great influence on her writing. As an editor, Fishbone has no equal.

Thisbe's parents taught her about deadlines and editing but they write academic books, so it's possible that nobody reads what they publish. Thisbe is determined to be both published and widely read by the time she is twenty-five.

From: Thisbe
To: Jason
Subject: Re: I'm thinking

Ooh, it's good! A couple of minor edits, if you wouldn't mind: (1) I am a Young Adult, not a "teen." (2) Please, please, please don't put in that comment about nobody reading my parents' books! And now you may continue. But first, here are my top picks for the stories we include:

A. The Tragedy of Elijah Sprout; my poem "Mightier Than the Sword"
B. The story about Gwendolyne La Bon-Bon (which I just found the courage to send you)
C. Your comments on whether or not a person is real or fictitious
D. A journal entry I wrote (and selected with extreme caution) about how my writing is like building a sand castle with wet sand. . . . I just sent it to you also.

From: Jason
To: Thisbe
Subject: Thisbe's technique

Those are great choices! I LOVED the story about Gwen. Poor Pearl and her sinuses. And I have made the changes you asked for. More coming through:

As an author, Thisbe relies heavily on autobiography. She also depends on many other kinds of texts, as well as finding inspiration in commercials, country songs, medieval fables, rants, and recipes. She occasionally shows her work to teachers but doesn't regard her writing as an "assignment." It's more of a mission: it's her "life's work," she says.

Thisbe spends a lot of time on her own, but it doesn't bother her. She enjoys her own company when she is working on a story, and says, "When you have an idea, you are never alone." We wish Thisbe every success in her future career.

For the back cover of the assignment:
Welcome to The Kingdom of Strange! There's only one monarch, but she is generous, imposing few rules and even less discipline on her subjects. Thisbe is very encouraging and loves to inspire her subjects, but if they run riot, she will not be held responsible. Who are the people of her kingdom, you ask?

Her words!

From: Thisbe
To: Jason
Subject: and for inside the front cover
How's this?

Dear Mr. Oliver,

This is Thisbe and Jason's assignment speaking. We have a question for you, and it is this: What kind of story are we? We thought we were a Young Adult novel, but now we are not so sure. Please answer this question, as it is weighing heavily upon us. We are sure that Thisbe and Jason would love to know, too.

Yours truly,

The Words

From: Jason
To: Thisbe
Subject: picture of me
Attachment: Jason1.jpeg
Excellent. Let's use it. And . . . if I may introduce myself properly
this time . . . My name is Jason. This is me. The real me.
What do you think? Is it—am I—acceptable?

From: Thisbe
To: Jason
Subject: picture of you . . .
Hmm. Let me think. Scroll down?
*
*
*
Bit more?
*
*
Ok, a bit more?
*
*
*
Yes.

THURSDAY

It is after midnight, and Thisbe's parents are comfortably settled in their comfortable bed. The telephone ringer is switched off, and Thisbe is in her room with Fishbone. Ed has taken Chutney out for a late walk and is now reading in the kitchen. Luggage and shoes still litter the hallway, and outerwear is hanging carelessly over the banisters. An umbrella leans against the front door at a precarious angle.

In the living room, a handmade greeting card stands on the coffee table bearing the late, hastily written but heartfelt note: "To Mom and Dad! Welcome back—I missed you so much. Love, Fiz xxx."

And now, I draw my hand away from the power button. I shove both my hands, palms together, between my knees as if I'm praying. I glance down at my recycling bin, full of printing mistakes and early drafts of my assignment. It's gone now, into Mr. Oliver's hands, adding to the mountain of assignments in his possession. But I don't care about grades this time. I learned a lot more than any of us expected while my parents were away. Maybe I'm beginning to see my dad's point about grades, after all?

I lean forward, looking at the screen. For a moment I turn to Fishbone, who is fast asleep on my bed. The fur is rising and falling on his warm tummy like prickles on a porcupine. It's really late, and I am tired but happy.

I lift my hands toward the keyboard like a pianist who knows, note for note, what kind of music she is going to play. I inhale deeply and count to four as I breathe out. My pinkie lands delicately on the shift key. I breathe. I type. I play my instrument and listen to the music of the keys. I play myself right back into The Kingdom of Strange and then, I lose myself in it.

"Why do I write?" I begin. I know the answer.

FRIDAY

Your Body in Mind
My teacher said
"Listen to your body"—
And so I did.

On the first day,
I listened to my body
And I heard silence.
I heard the noise of traffic.
I heard the telephone ringing.
I heard the radio
And the falling rain.

On the second day,
I listened to my body again.
This time I heard pain.

On the third day,
I listened to my body and
Heard sorrow.

On the fourth day,
I listened again.
This time I heard words.

And on the fifth day,
I listened with all my might
And I heard music.

Thisbe's NEW AND IMPROVED
Top 10 List of Things I Love
(in no particular order)

1. Swimming with Granny Ed—swimsuit optional (for Granny, NOT me)
2. Swimming alone—swimsuit definitely required
3. Getting feedback on my poems from Jason
4. Fishbone demonstrating Cat Pose
5. The smell of nutmeg combined with fresh autumn leaves, a.k.a. Aroma De Chutney
6. David's mischievous smile when he talks about his grandfather
7. The healing powers of cheesecake
8. Knowing where my father gets his sense of humor from. And not minding at all.
9. My hands
10. The secret recipe for Grandpa Michael's apple pancakes, which is now stored safely in the deepest chamber of my heart. Mom and Dad will have pancakes for breakfast tomorrow.

THE END

SHULA KLINGER was born in St. Albans, England. Her poetry, journalism, and creative non-fiction have been published in the UK, the US, and Canada. She holds an undergraduate degree in English from Oxford University and a Masters in Educational Technology from Cambridge. Before moving to Canada, Shula worked in children's book publishing and for a multimedia division of the BBC.

Since completing her Ph.D. at the University of British Columbia, Shula has mentored teachers and developed online course materials for schools in British Columbia. While working for the Vancouver School Board, she also created and moderated "The Attic," an online community for students who love reading and writing. She now works as a consultant in online education for schools throughout the province. She is also the developer and moderator of Wordspace, an online domain for young writers.

Shula lives in Richmond, BC, with her husband, Graham, their son, Benjamin, and Moby the dachshund.

The Kingdom of Strange is her first novel. Visit her online at: **www.shulaklinger.com**